I0604726

SEASHIMMER'S CHOICE

Book 1 of the Seashimmer Chronicles

WENDY METCALFE

Copyright © 2025 Wendy Metcalfe

Wendy Metcalfe has asserted her right under the Copyright, Designs and Patents Act 1988 to be identified as the author of this work.

This book is sold subject to the condition that it shall not, by way of trade or otherwise, be lent, resold, hired out, or otherwise circulated without the publisher's prior consent in any form of binding or cover other than that in which it is published and without similar condition including this condition being imposed on the subject purchaser.

All the characters in this publication are fictional and any resemblance to real persons, living or dead, is purely coincidental.

No AI (Artificial Intelligence) has been used in the writing of this publication. Without in any way limiting the author's exclusive rights under copyright, any use of this publication to 'train' generative artificial intelligence (AI) technologies to generate text is expressly prohibited. The author reserves all rights to licence uses of this work for generative AI training and development of machine language learning models

First published in the United Kingdom 2025 by Wendy Metcalfe

CHAPTER ONE

Danetha Windhammer watched her footing as she crossed the deck. She was aboard the family lizardship *Iceforged*. He was a three-master, and they had too much sail up for this blow.

The ship was a few days out of Magnar Harbour, on the coast of the Southern Dominion. They were riding the Southern Island Current towards the Marisol Isles. The winds were usually steady at this season, but at Forenoon Watch an unexpected storm had blown up. Danetha had been dragged from her bed to help reduce sail.

She was a wealthy dwarf Trader's elder daughter, but she dressed like a common deckhand. She had cut her dark brown hair to the level of her jaw several years ago. It had been the first of Danetha's rebellions against her mother's plans for her.

The voice of the Captain, her father Kiboth, came to her from the foredeck. "Can you not stop this blow, *Iceforged*?" he shouted.

The ship's figurehead turned and looked down on him. His visage was that of a noble dwarf, with hair swept back off his brow, and a neat pointed beard. He wore a heavy cloak which swathed his torso. His magic gave him a permanently frosty look, and made him appear to be clad in silver.

"I am doing my best, Captain," the ship replied. "Even lizardship magic has its limits. My power cannot defeat the ocean. And it is angry today."

Danetha had been aboard *Iceforged* since she was ten years old, and had many years' experience of handling the ship. She took up her station by the mainmast, ready to haul on the sheet. The deck pitched and rolled beneath her feet, and the heightening waves foamed white as they crashed over the bowsprit.

Her best friend Sammol Blackwind was beside her. They were opposites in all ways; Danetha's family wealthy, Sammol's less so. Danetha's face was white as the winter moon. Sammol's features were black as the moonless night.

Skylar Icecracker shuffled into place on the other side of the mainmast. The Sailmaster was not the best she had met, and had made life very hard for her when she first came aboard. He had been out to prove that the Captain's daughter would not make a good sailor. She had set out to prove him wrong, and had succeeded.

Recently his harshness had returned, and Danetha suspected that was Kiboth's doing. Her father wished to persuade her to leave *Iceforged*. She had refused to do so.

"Haul!" Skylar gave the command and Danetha lent

her strength to the rest of her team to grasp the thick sheet and ease the sail down the mast. They were the first sail set, and that gave her great satisfaction. Let her father tell her she wasn't an efficient sailor now. He would have to try harder than that to justify taking her off *Iceforged*.

Now the ship pitched less, but the spray and cold wind still whipped across the deck. "Let us get out of this cold," she said to Sammol. "A cup of hot tea would be welcome now."

"That it would," he replied.

They clattered down the gangway to the mid-deck, their boots raising a hollow thud on the timbers. Lizardwood was far more durable than any other wood the shipwrights used. Lizardships endured for many generations, while the hardest hardwood tree ships rotted and failed.

The galley was busy with the rest of their watch. Having been woken from their beds, all needed warmth and sustenance before seeking their slumbers again. Danetha poured a mug of tea from the kettle suspended on its hook. Garil was the cook on duty, and had brewed a new kettle as soon as the order to stand down was given. The old dwarf had skin of polished mahogany, the nearest anyone on *Iceforged's* permanent crew came to having black skin.

She thanked him for his foresight, and went to join Sammol on the end of the table. There was always a gap between the crew and Sammol. They were happy to give him orders, but not to be his friend.

Danetha curled her chilled hands around her warm mug and took a sip of the tea. Her eyes widened in surprise. This was not the usual rough Kavit blend, but taken from the ship's precious stores of best Arylin leaf. It had the subtle but delicate taste of honey, and the hint of a scent of southern blossoms.

Her father would chastise Garil for this later. The old cook would shrug off the reprimand, as he had thousands of others. Garil knew what made a happy ship. Sometimes better than her father.

She drank in silence, and as soon as she was finished departed for her cabin. Sammol left the galley then too. Danetha did not miss the unfriendly gazes of the crew as he passed them. She had the privilege of her own cabin here. Sammol was bunked in what used to be a store. He slept alone too.

"It is for his safety," Kiboth had said when he made the arrangement. Danetha had thought it was rather more to avoid Sammol 'corrupting' the ship's crew. Her father was more than willing to make use of Sammol's strong back and excellent sailing skills, but rather less willing to acknowledge his equal status.

She had become Sammol's friend the moment she had heard that he too desired no children, and found the idea of joining his body to another's just as distasteful as she did. With Sammol she knew she was always safe.

Sammol was a 'prentice, and Danetha lived in dread for the day Kiboth considered Sammol's 'prenticeship complete, and threw him off the ship. There was no prospect of Sammol ever joining the ship's crew as a deckhand.

She reached her cabin and opened the door. "Good sleep, Sammol," she wished him. He nodded, and passed on by. Danetha went inside quickly, shutting the door on his retreating back. She did not wish to see his lonely figure stride down the cramped access to his tiny prison. He did not wear a slave's collar or mark, but he might as well have done, for all the respect he garnered from the ship's crew.

She took off her boots and sank onto her bunk. She had long ago learned to sleep at any hour, and instantly oblivion took her.

She woke before eight bells, and went to the galley to down a mug of tea– the rough Kavit blend this time – and eat a dish of hearty porridge for sustenance. The storm had blown itself out. The deck was level, barely moving beneath her feet.

She finished her breakfast as eight bells sounded, and came

up on deck in time to hear the Officer of the Watch's report. The storm had died down some hours ago, and the Southern Island Current was steady in its course again. She knew that would not last much longer. The first smudges of the Marisol Isles were visible on the horizon. Soon the ship would near the Zellen Race, and all crew would be needed on deck again.

But for this moment, Danetha had nothing to do but trim sail. They had been set efficiently by the opposite watch, and for now most needed no tending. The day was bright, and soon the noon sight would be done.

She looked towards the bow. Ice's head was washed with gold from Yareli's rays, showing off the waves of his thick hair. His head turned from side to side as the ship sliced through the water. His features were somewhat between the smooth flesh of a dwarf and the harsher angles of carved wood.

Danetha picked her way carefully between the coiled ropes and chests, and came up beside the figurehead. "How is the race?" she asked.

"Quiet, for once." His deep voice did not carry its usual calm. "Danetha, I am concerned about the Captain. My senses tell me he is failing. He feigns strength, but I can see he has none."

She thrust down her panic. Kiboth's coughing fits had started two years ago, and each winter they grew worse. He tried to spend most of his time sailing the warm waters of the Southern Dominion, but even owning a lizardship had not made him one of the most desired Traders to deal with. Often he was forced back to the coast of the Northern Alliance, with its chill, wet winters.

"I do not want to think about that," she said.

The figurehead looked down at her. His grey eyes skewered her, their gaze the look of one with many generations of experience. "You must. Plan carefully, Danetha. Both you and Sammol are at risk when Kiboth dies."

"What do you mean?"

"We will talk of this later." A warning note was in the figurehead's voice. Now Danetha heard the thud of feet coming towards her. They had a distinctive one-two gait, the sound of a person with a limp.

"What are you doing bothering my ship?" Kiboth's voice was rough.

She turned to face him. "The sails did not require tending for a moment, so I came to view the approaches."

"More likely to poison the mind of my lizardship. Back to your post, sailor."

Danetha flinched at his words. Her father had never been affectionate to her in the way he was with her brothers, but to rebuke his daughter as a common sailor...

She stepped past him and returned to her post at the mainmast. Umutt was waiting there, and she braced for another rebuke from the First Mate. It did not come.

"Your father is ill," he said quietly. "It has made his mood bleak. I will be seeking out Thonar Bonehealer as soon as we make port at Sang."

"I would prefer he saw Mergild Armsetter. She at least knows her profession."

Umutt sighed, and she saw weariness in the old dwarf's blue eyes. "We would all rather your father did not have his prejudices," he said. She stared at him. For a First Mate to criticise his captain was unheard of. Yet she knew Umutt was loyal to Kiboth. "I cannot go against my Captain's wishes, even if those wishes might hasten his death."

"You think he might die here?" Fear made Danetha's voice wobble.

"I think the help of your Aunt Avora will be needed to prevent that."

"I will go and fetch her the moment we heave to," she said.

There was no more time for talk. The ship was approaching the Zellen Race, and it was time to furl sail. Danetha's arms ached with the repeated hauling and furling of sails. Everyone would be glad to get into port and rest.

The crew finished furling sails as the old navigator Gundur Windspeaker stepped up beside the figurehead. They were bound for the port of Sang this day, and Gundur would guide them in. The next hours were filled with setting and re-setting sails for their approach to the harbour. By the time *Iceforged* nudged up to the quay Danetha felt her usual exhaustion.

In the frenzy of getting the ship into her berth she had not noticed that her father was absent from the deck. That was not usual.

Umutt came to her side. "I will send Skylar to summon Thonar Bonehealer. We will be lodging at the Resthouse, whatever your father's objections. Find your Aunt Avora and bring her there. Tell her it is a worsening of the usual trouble."

The lines were secured to the quay, and Sammol joined the crew to heave the gangplank into place. Its heavy end thudded onto the cobbles of the quay. They had been fortunate to secure a berth right on the quayside, and the Mariner's Guild Resthouse was opposite their berth.

"Go," Umutt said to Danetha the moment the gangplank was set.

"May I take Sammol with me?" she asked. She hated having to ask that, but she had been bothered by unsavoury attention here before.

"You may," Umutt replied.

"Thank you." Danetha turned to her friend. "We are going to find Aunt Avora," she told him. He nodded but said nothing, following her down the gangplank.

She set foot on the quay and turned to her right. She wore her lightest breeches and shirt, but still sweat slicked her back.

They rounded the end of the Resthouse and started the climb up the road. The sweat on Danetha's back was sticky. This was a discomfort she would never be able to live with.

What had made her think of that? Her home was in Dimiel, on the southern coast of the Northern Alliance. The sprawling old house on the headland above the harbour had been handed down through the Windhammers for five generations.

But things would be mightily changed upon Kiboth's death. And however much she might wish to deny it, in her heart, Danetha knew that his end was near.

CHAPTER TWO

The thought of her father's impending demise put urgency into Danetha's steps. She reached the narrow street of high buildings which ran along the back of the Resthouse, and turned along it. Avora's apartment was on the top story of a handsome building part-way down the street. She reached it and opened the gate which gave access to the garden beyond, and the stairs.

Sammol had hung back at the entrance, and she turned to him and said, "Follow me." Was her friend reluctant to enter this fine building? Over the years they had sailed together she had become attuned to his feelings about his family's station. The Blackwinds were fine sailors and Traders, but the darkness of their skin encouraged some Merchants to place their business elsewhere.

Still, Sammol's father was a member of the Mariner's Guild. They had not excluded him, like they had tried to do to several female captains.

Danetha climbed the steps to the upper level, her boots thudding on the heavy timbers. She came out onto the balcony which gave a view over the lush garden. She walked to her left until she came to the door with the ornate number one affixed to it. As she was about to knock on the door it

11

opened.

Aunt Avora greeted Danetha with a smile. Her pale skin was framed by long wavy white hair. She was dressed in light breeches and a short-sleeved smock. "I saw that *Iceforged* was in port," she said. "How bad is your father?"

Danetha was startled by her Aunt's words. How did she know that her father was ill? "Umutt said to tell you that it is a worsening of the usual trouble."

Avora nodded, as if that was the answer she'd expected. "Then we will need my herbs." She reached behind her, to the hide pack placed ready in the hallway, and hauled it over her shoulders.

"Umutt said Kiboth would be at the Resthouse."

"Umutt has sense," Avora replied. "Let us hurry." She closed the door and led them down the stairs. "Has a physician been called?"

"Thonar Bonehealer," Danetha replied.

Her aunt's only response to that was a grunt. It confirmed Danetha's suspicion that Thonar was a quack. If I were ill I would want the best care I could buy, she thought, whether that skill was wielded by a man's or a woman's hand. What stupidity was a prejudice which might hasten your death.

They reached the Resthouse in swift time, Avora

striding out along the cobbles of the quay. When they arrived in the fine timbered lobby of the building it was to learn that Kiboth had arrived mere minutes before.

"Stupid man," Avora muttered. "He has an excellent and trustworthy crew, yet he lingers to see to the cargo."

Danetha was shocked by her aunt's words, then realised she was right. She applied herself to the task at hand and approached the desk built of intricate wooden layers, with its greeter in traditional dark blue sailor's uniform behind it. She drew herself up and said, "I am Danetha Windhammer. I must know where my father is lodged." Her mother had taught her this imperious voice. At the time Danetha had thought it silly, now she understood its value.

"Kiboth Windhammer is in Shipmaster One," the man replied.

So her father must be really ill if he had let Umutt argue him into paying for the best suite of rooms in the Resthouse.

"We will go there now," she said. Her tone allowed for no argument.

"I know the way," Avora said, and made for the stairway in the far corner of the lobby. Danetha followed, turning to beckon a reluctant Sammol to follow them up.

Danetha did not relish more climbing in this heat, but as she moved upwards she felt the cool touch of air on her face.

The building had wide windows at every level, their situation on the southern and northern walls allowing a constant flow of air though. The substantial wooden overhang on the southern roof shaded the space from the glare of the harsh southern rays.

They climbed to the second level, and the air cooled around Danetha again. Umutt had stationed the youngest member of *Iceforged's* crew at the outer door of the rooms, no doubt to keep out unwanted guests. He looked nervous at their approach. Sammol took himself off along the hallway, to settle on one of the benches further along the wall. Danetha let Avora lead the way to Kiboth.

"The physician is with him now," the crewman said.

Danetha heard the unspoken message. Her aunt would not be welcome in the room with the man.

Avora took the news calmly. "Then we shall wait here," she said. She made for the nearest bench and sat down. Danetha followed her aunt and plonked down beside her. "He might be dying," she protested.

Avora turned and studied her. Danetha noticed that the lines on her aunt's face had increased since her last visit, but her white hair was just as luxuriant as ever. Avora had turned white at an unusually young age, and it had proved a useful weapon to discourage unwanted male attention.

Danetha wondered how soon she could adopt a Crone persona and be ignored.

"How is Okrene?" Avora asked.

"My mother is as insistent as ever that I must leave *Iceforged*. I fear she has plans to Present me this next Season."

Avora's lips twitched. "I am thinking you would not be in favour of such a move?"

"Your thought is right."

Avora gave her a searching stare. "Danetha, the time for pleasantries is past. We both know your father is not long for this world. You must give serious thought to what you will do when he is gone."

"I am the eldest. I will inherit *Iceforged*, and sail the oceans."

"That is what should happen." Avora's words were cautious. "But Okrene is a devious one. I advise you to have other plans if things do not work out that way."

CHAPTER THREE

Danetha stared at her aunt. She had never even considered the idea that *Iceforged* would not come to her. Her eldest brother Thatnog was no sailor. He had only been aboard the lizardship a handful of times, and even on that short acquaintance he had upset the crew.

"Ice would never allow that," she said.

Avora gave her another of those looks which made Danetha want to fidget. Her aunt's deep blue eyes seemed to see right into her soul. "Just heed my words," she said.

Danetha wanted to question her more, but at that moment Thonar Bonehealer emerged from Kiboth's rooms. He saw Avora, gave her a scowl, and departed.

"And now he is gone, perhaps I can do some good," her Aunt said, and stood up.

Danetha followed her into Kiboth's rooms. Her father lay on the bed, looking out to the ocean. Danetha had not noticed before how shrunken he had become. He was wasting away.

But most distressing was his constant coughing. The fits lasted long minutes, and left Kiboth lying weakly against his pillows when they passed.

Avora took her bag into the small cooking area beyond

the archway, and heated a kettle of water. While it boiled she took a jar of golden liquid from her pack and retrieved a spoon from a drawer. "This is pure honey," she told Kiboth. "It will ease the roughness of your throat. It has the healing power of the wildflowers of Elain."

Kiboth made the effort to sit up, and Avora got the honey into him. "That is good," she said when he had not coughed for some minutes. She went to tend the kettle, returning with a mariner's mug of liquid. "Drink this as often as the seizures come," she said, and put it down on the chest beside him.

Kiboth made no response to her, but his hand reached out to grasp the mug. He took several long sips from it. "That is better," Avora said. "My prescription now is sleep. All ship crews are impoverished in that regard by the time they reach port."

Kiboth's eyes drooped, and Avora gestured to Danetha to leave the room. They came out into the hallway, and Avora steered Danetha along it, away from the crewman's listening ears.

"I believe your father will pull through this time," she said. "But when you return to winter in northern climes that good may be undone. Think hard on what I told you, Danetha. You are far too clever to be trapped as the wife of a wealthy Merchant. Have other plans for your life."

Avora tended Kiboth for several days before he was strong enough to return to *Iceforged*. Danetha spent that time running between the ship and the Resthouse, and the last two days helping to find a suitable cargo for the ship.

She accompanied Umutt to the Guildhouse, and was treated to the worst discourtesy she had ever encountered.

Their cargo was unexciting. Farming implements sat alongside cooking pots and eating utensils in the holds. Umutt had wanted to transport some of the southern isles' beautiful goldwork fabrics, but no Merchant would entrust them with their passage. By the time *Iceforged* was ready to sail Danetha's spirits were thoroughly depressed.

They left Sang on a bright morn, and soon picked up the Southern Island Current. The wind and ocean ran true, and took them in swift time past the Irani and Elain Isles.

The ship lost the current at First Watch. The seas were rough where the Island Current met the Marisol Current. The combination of a black night without the illumination of the moon Palemon, and the unpredictable swells, made for some very hard sailing. It was Morning Watch before the Marisol Current took them swiftly northwards and away from the chaos of clashing winds and waves. The watch system had long ago been thoroughly disrupted, and Danetha was tired enough to sleep on her feet.

Iceforged made his way steadily northwards, and the days passed in the usual routines of raising, furling, and trimming sail. Danetha did not miss the fact that her father rarely completed an entire watch on deck. The ship and her crew could manage perfectly well without him.

As they approached the coast of the Northern Alliance Danetha had a rare slack moment. After the chaos of the all-crew-on-deck periods, Sammol had found himself rostered to the opposite watch. But now, today, he was on her watch again.

Sammol understood exactly how she felt. He had saved her from the attentions of many males, often to his own detriment. The vilest had uttered obscenities about the contamination of her body from his flesh.

No person should have to suffer that, Danetha thought. She had plans to challenge many such things when she was captain of *Iceforged*.

When, not if. Her talks with Aunt Avora had finally got her to accept that Kiboth would not live much longer. Her aunt had urged her to pay close attention to her mother's doings.

"For when Kiboth is gone there will no longer be any

checks on her actions," Avora had said. It had sounded like a prophecy of doom to Danetha.

She was thinking of such things as she came up on deck for Forenoon Watch. They had left the tropics behind many days ago, and the weather was noticeably cooler. They were in the northern climes now, and autumn was calling.

Danetha could sense the subtle changes of climate. Years of sailing the oceans had attuned her to the touch of the winds on her face, the smell of the ocean in its different guises. Her face and her nose told her that winter would not be long in coming in these parts.

As she came up on deck she saw Sammol there, and her father was absent again. She was about to take up her position by the mainmast when the figurehead turned towards them. "I desire a word, Danetha, Sammol," he said. "Come close."

Danetha hesitated, but Umutt was in command this watch, and said, "Go and talk to *Iceforged*. When a figurehead calls you, you obey."

That was an unfamiliar perspective. As a young woman she had gone to talk to him whenever she wanted. She had slowly learned when her attentions were unwanted, but the idea of being summoned by him had never occurred to her.

She had been taught, as every lizardship sailor was, that she must never touch the figurehead. They were trapped creatures, and breaking the boundaries of their space could result in death if the ship decided to roll and kill you as a result.

When she reached the figurehead *Iceforged* looked down at her. Then he did something he had never done before. He extended his hand towards her. Hesitantly, she reached forward and grasped the ship's hand. The flesh felt like smoothly-planed wood warmed in the sun. The lizardship's fingers curled around hers.

"It is time for warnings," *Iceforged* said. "My captain plans to put you and Sammol ashore when we return to Dimiel. Your father has finally given in to your mother's demands to have you Presented."

"I will not be Matched!" Danetha snarled as Sammol came up beside her.

"He also plans to terminate Sammol's 'prenticeship," the figurehead said.

"That has been feared for some time," Danetha replied.

"This last piece of information I now give you must be kept to you and Sammol alone. As we round Oslen Headland you will see a deep, shadowed cave entrance. It is home to the lizardship *Seashimmer*."

"Why has no-one ever discovered it?" she asked.

"Her. She has beached well into the cave. She used her magic to ask the ocean to carry her in, out of view of the greedy and voracious who would see owning a lizardship as the way to their fortune."

Danetha barked a bitter laugh. "A look at the way we are treated should disabuse them of that."

"You two-legs do find fine ways to hate each other."

The grip of his hand tightened, and Danetha became alarmed. "I wish you for my Captain. But if you are denied my Captainship, remember *Seashimmer*. Beware of your mother, Danetha. And next time you are in Sang, ask Avora who she really is."

He released her hand and beckoned Sammol forwards. Her friend stepped to the figurehead, and to Danetha's surprise, Ice took his hand too. She felt pride – and jealousy – for that. She made her way back to the foremast, letting the figurehead talk to her friend in private.

Umutt stood by the mast. His face held a thoughtful expression. "*Iceforged* has never touched the Captain," he said quietly. "You are honoured."

"Even so, our continuance on board is in doubt," she

said.

Umutt's eyes took on a sad expression. "You must realise that Kiboth has not much longer in this world. I should not say this, but I wish you to escape your mother's clutches. You deserve more than a dreary Match to a rich Trader. Plan your future well, Danetha."

CHAPTER FOUR

Danetha had never expected the gruff First Mate to speak so freely or so honestly. She wanted him to say more about his thoughts, but before she could ask, Skylar roared a command to furl sail, and she scrambled to her position.

The next hours were full of furling, raising, and trimming sail. The ocean was rough where the Northern Current broke on the headland, its waters clashing with those of the Petros Current moving in from the east. Danetha had known days when the clash was so severe that they had dropped anchor a way off the headland, to sit and wait out a dangerous blow.

Today it was not so dangerous, and after furling sail her watch was stood down, and she went gratefully to her bunk to sleep.

While she slept *Iceforged* sailed steadily closer to the headland of the Northern Alliance, and when Danetha came back on watch it was close. The land dropped away here in sheer white-stone cliffs, which no mariner could miss as a landmark.

At great distance, the white face of the rocks appeared as a smooth slab. But as the lizardship sailed closer the mass of angles and fissures and jagged planes became visible. Danetha knew some daredevils had climbed that face, but she did not wish to.

As the lizardship neared the headland she took position on the starboard side of the mainmast. When *Iceforged* turned north-west onto the Petros Current she would be well-placed to see the cave where the *Seashimmer* supposedly lay.

She found it hard to believe that such a precious treasure as a lizardship could lie hidden there. Surely some bold adventurer had explored all the caves along that, admittedly rough, coastline? Perhaps the lizardship had used her magic to raise the seas and the mists to drive the curious away. She would not find it easy to reach it – if she needed to.

It would not come to that. *Iceforged* was hers by right. She could look forward to putting in place all the changes she had wanted to make for years when she came aboard as Captain.

It was twilight by the time they had negotiated the last course change to bring the lizardship onto the Petros Current. As they passed the *Seashimmer's* supposed resting place all Danetha could see was a black hole leading into the cliff. It was certainly large enough to accommodate a lizardship, but Danetha could see no sign of her. She would have to discover whether there was some way down to the cave from the clifftop.

She was certain now that Kiboth would not sail another

voyage. He was still in his cabin when he would normally be on deck, fussing over Gundur. Danetha thought the old Navigator would be relieved at the absence of his captain.

Men and their egos! *Iceforged* would be very different with her in command.

She had no more time for rumination as the Petros Current slacked and the crew began the process of re-setting the sails. She lost herself in the rhythms of tending the ship. She was trying not to think about what awaited her at the end of this voyage. She was always reluctant to go ashore and face her Mother these days. Most often their meetings ended in disagreement.

Iceforged rounded the breakwater, and took her usual berth by the quay. In the frenzy of managing sails and anchors, Danetha did not notice that her father was still absent. He never missed being on deck when the lizardship approached her home port. It deepened her feeling that he would not sail again.

Umutt detailed Berovar to take the manifest to the Mariner's Guild to arrange for the unloading of their cargo. Most of it was heavy, being made of metals, and the farming implements were bulky and of awkward shapes. Stowing them had been tedious enough, but hauling them out of the holds would be worse.

Berovar returned in short order, accompanied by six stevedores wearing an unfamiliar uniform. No doubt they were employed by the Merchant who had paid for transport, who wished to ensure that he received all his goods.

She stepped back out of the way at the first creak of the loading arm on the dock. It swung over *Iceforged's* deck as Orik Hallandor removed the hold's hatch cover. The white-complexioned human Cargomaster was tall and solid, and stevedores did not argue with him. He had served on *Iceforged* for many years.

Danetha joined the crew to slip the ropes around the cargo and secure the knots for lifting. Then they retreated to the deck as the loading arm swung the awkwardly-shaped pieces over to the dock. The stevedores took charge of them then, loading the goods into wheeled carts which they pushed into the Bondhouse across the quay.

As Danetha watched the first load disappear inside the Bondhouse Umutt approached her. "Your mother has summoned you," he said. "The Captain is already at home. She wishes to speak with you."

Danetha sighed, and turned to Sammol. "I suppose it cannot be put off any longer."

"I will wait at home for your news," he said.

Reluctantly, Danetha left *Iceforged* and her friend behind, trying to ignore the looks of the crew as they watched her walk along the quay. She had never been sure how she felt about her father. He had always favoured Thatnog - spoiled him, if she was honest. She thought back to Kiboth's rebuke at the Marisol Isles, where he had called her a common sailor. Was that all she was to him? It filled her with fear for the future.

She turned west and left the quay at her back, climbing the path to Truesilver View, the broad road where the first row of Trader's houses were situated. The most desirable properties faced the sea. All stood apart from each other, and were generations old. Some were constructed of black stone expensively shipped in from the far west coast of the Northern Alliance. Others were made of pale cream blocks, quarried locally.

The Windhammer house was the last on the row facing the ocean. It was one of the pale stone buildings. The house was surrounded by substantial gardens. Danetha's mother spent much time there in the warmer months, tending her overblown loveflowers. The gardens had a sickly feminine feel with many pink flowers, which Danetha hated. If she were one day to inherit the house, her first act would be to rip up those loveflowers by their roots.

Her mother was one of those stupid women who believed in romance. Danetha thought that was an idea invented by women to disguise the brutal fact that they were wombs on legs, their bodies existing merely for the satisfaction of male lust. That was a role Danetha never intended to accept.

As she approached the elaborate wrought-iron gate to the front garden she saw a windcar parked outside the house, its sails idly flapping. Her misgivings rose. She had a good idea who the car belonged to. Her suspicions were confirmed when the portly form of Dalgion Truespeaker bustled down the garden path and into the road. She turned her back on the lawyer, and opened the gate. Kiboth must be bad if he had consented to spend good money on that man's services. He had a natural resistance to lawyers.

She strode to the front door. She had never had a key to the house, being away on *Iceforged* most of the time. Now she wondered if that was another sign of her mother's power.

The front door opened as she reached it, revealing her mother dressed in a black silk gown. Several emotions assaulted Danetha. Her father must be bad if Okrene had changed into her mourning gown. But the thing which bothered her most was the fine beadwork on the dress. Expensive black crystals winked and flashed in the light. They made intricate floral patterns on the bodice, sleeves, and hem of the gown. It must have cost a pretty amount of gold, and would have taken weeks to make. Was Okrene... relishing Kiboth's death?

"Hurry, my daughter. Your father is waiting for you." There was a gleam of something unpleasant in her mother's eyes. Was it triumph? Had Okrene been waiting for Kiboth to die? There was certainly no sign that her mother would miss Kiboth when he had breathed his last.

Those were unsettling thoughts, and Danetha thrust them aside and stepped into the handsome hallway, with its redwood-panelled walls and white marble floor. A new tapestry adorned the one long wall, an intricately-worked scene of The Marriage of Algion and Gilvora. Danetha wondered what message her mother wanted to send by that. Gilvora had never wanted that Match, and had hung herself a year later. Was the tapestry a warning?

Feeling further unsettled, she followed her mother up the fine hardwood carved staircase. At the landing they did not turn into the large marital bedroom with its wide widows and fine view of the ocean, but went to the rear of the house.

Kiboth had been settled into the best guest room, which overlooked the large garden. Its vegetation was drab at this season, dying back for winter. What cruelty was this to deny her father his last view of the ocean?

When Danetha looked on Kiboth's shrunken form she had no doubt that it would be his last day in this life. He coughed repeatedly, and looked so thin that he bore no resemblance to the hale father she knew who could topple a half-grown ox off its feet.

Kiboth raised a weak hand and beckoned her forward. She approached the bed, and he took her hand. His flesh was hot with fever, and the grip of his fingers weak. "I am sorry," he mumbled.

"Sorry for what, father?" she asked.

"Everything."

His grip on her loosened. His hand flopped back onto the bed. Danetha's heart missed a beat. He was dying. She watched the man who had once been so strong take his last, rattling breaths, and lie still.

"So, it is over," Okrene said. "I will send for Rantin Sorrowbearer."

Danetha studied her mother's face. There was no sign of tears there, nor even any hint of sadness. What Danetha read there was relief – and perhaps joy – at her release.

She turned from Okrene to go to her own room. She needed time to think, to come to terms with this loss. And time to plan. She was sure Okrene had some scheme for her which she would not like.

An hour later she had cried herself out and considered her options. Most were unpalatable, and she hoped she would not need the plans she had made. She must face whatever Okrene had in store for her now. She needed to be aware of her mother's scheming.

She changed into the new thick soft blue breeches and tunic she had bought a year ago in Kenaz. The town, just inland from the far eastern headland of the Northern Alliance, was famed for its fine cloth and beautiful dyed fabrics. *Iceforged* had sailed a difficult passage there in midwinter when other ships refused to put out, and had earned a handsome bonus for the trip. She had used some of that to buy these practical winter clothes.

She descended the staircase and found her mother in the formal drawing room. She hated the ornate goldwork and the fussiness of this room, but it was the centre of her mother's domain.

Okrene sat in the gilded chair she favoured and beckoned Danetha to sit with her at the table. "I am disappointed you have chosen to wear those ugly clothes, my daughter," she said.

Danetha's anger surged. "My father has just died, and

all you choose to do is chastise me for my dress!"

"Now that you are no longer aboard *Iceforged* you will have to foreswear your sailor's life. You will become the dutiful daughter I require. To that end, I persuaded Kiboth to sign a new Deed of Intention this morn. *Iceforged* will now pass to Thatnog."

CHAPTER FIVE

Okrene's words had been half-expected, but still they landed like cold lumps in Danetha's belly. So that was why her father had been sorry.

"I have had discussions with the Goldbows," Okrene continued. "Befril desires a new wife, and you would fit him well."

Danetha stared at her mother. "How dare you! How dare you try to force me to provide pleasures of the flesh for that fat slob! He is a disgusting man."

"He is a very rich man. Your dowry would place the Windhammers onto a very secure financial footing."

"You vicious old witch! I will not be a pawn in your evil scheme."

"Danetha, you must see sense. In recent years our wealth has dwindled away. We barely have the funds to maintain this house now. We need the money Befril would bring."

"Perhaps if you had not spent unnecessary gold on that obscene mourning dress we would not be in such a position," Danetha snarled. "You shall not get your wish, mother."

She rose to her feet and marched out of the room. Her

course now was clear. Her mother's summons rang in her ears. She ignored it. She would not be prey to any of Okrene's schemes.

Anger, grief, and shock mingled in her and gave her a surge of new strength. Her thoughts were clear now, even if her body still ached from hauling sail. The pack she had half-filled before her interview with her mother lay on her bed. The clothes Danetha had selected to fill it were practical breeches and tunics, and her spare pair of boots. The gowns and cloaks her mother had bought for her over the last two years were left in the wardrobe. She slipped a hide jerkin with several pockets on over her tunic, and resumed her preparations.

Running a finger under the drawer in her mirror table, she released the latch on the hidden compartment in the bottom of the drawer. Inside lay a hide bag heavy with coins. She lifted it out and tucked it into the inside pocket of her jerkin. This bag contained her wages and bonuses for the last three years of sailing on *Iceforged*. She had saved every coin of it for a day like this.

Peering out of the window, she saw it was now fully dark. It was hard to see anything beyond the illumination of the room. She was sure her mother would summon Rantin Sorrowbearer swiftly to remove Kiboth's body. Danetha was of the opinion that her mother was keen to be rid of all traces of her father as soon as could be.

The mortician arrived an hour later, and Danetha heard the voices of him and his assistant, and the shriller tones of her mother directing them to the guest room. As they disappeared inside she opened the door of her room, hefted her pack onto her back, and made her way quietly down the staircase.

She had long ago perfected the art of sneaking silently and unseen from the house, and those skills came into use again this night. The heavy jacket she wore was dyed black, and she moved like a silent shadow through the rooms to the garden door.

There she stopped to pull on and lace her heavy winter boots before quietly opening the door. The night was chill, and she fastened up her winter storm jacket. She eased the door open and slipped outside, into the shadowy garden, clicking the door quietly shut behind her.

She stopped and listened for a moment. The voices were descending the main staircase. She would not be missed for some while yet. She took three paces to her right, then stepped forward until she heard the quiet crunch of the loose stone path under her boots. The garden was in complete darkness, and she must cross it using only her memory of the space.

The path ran straight, and she followed it to the centre of the garden. Her boot kicked the low stone wall bounding the fountain of Ruli and Balga, the Lovers of Lochlainn, which dominated the centre of the garden. The ornate thing was hideous in Danetha's opinion, and was another thing that would be swiftly removed if she ever inherited the house.

She turned to her left and navigated the semicircle of path that bounded the fountain until her feet found the rough stone of the straight path on its other side. Quietly she strode along it.

The path ended at a gate which led out into the road. She opened it, relieved that someone had oiled the hinges recently and the gate made no noise. She slipped through and closed it. She had walked this route in both the light and on the darkest night, and the lack of illumination here did not bother her. Occasionally they were plagued by burglars and cutthroats in these parts, but Danetha rather thought the brisk cold wind from the north and the serious chill of this night would deter most.

Her feet found the cobbled road, and she walked north, past the end of the second row of Trader's houses. They were occupied by families with less grand reputations than her own. She kept on going north, past the end of the third row of houses, then turned east along the road behind them. These dwellings were occupied by the least wealthy Traders, and had no view of the ocean.

The road here was rough, and she walked slowly along it, feeling each step. Sammol's family had their house on this third row, of course. Fully half the houses on the row were occupied by people with darker complexions. Danetha had never thought on that before, but now she wondered why it was that matters were arranged that way.

She walked along the rough road until she reached the easternmost house. This was the Blackwind home. The gate into their back garden did creak when she opened it, and she hoped no-one would come to investigate the noise. Sammol's family garden was not grand like the Windhammers, and she had no fear of destroying anything precious as she trampled through the wet and tangled grasses.

She knew that Sammol's room was on the ground floor, and overlooked this garden. Sammol was the youngest of three brothers. The eldest, Thanulin, was about to be Matched to Mendiel Blackbow. The Blackbows owned mines in Bansuru, and Danetha wondered how Sammol's mother Rura had made such a good match.

Sammol's middle brother Buzum sailed the family's

Tradeship, *Darksilver*. The ship was a sturdy enough craft, but it was not a lizardship.

As Danetha approached Sammol's room she had a rush of doubt. Would he want to see her? She swallowed hard, and took another step forward. He would not know that Kiboth was dead. She must tell him that, at least.

She reached the window and knocked on it in sailor's code, spelling out her name. The room had a door out into the garden, and she waited by it. She was about to knock on the window again when the door grated open. She could see little of the room beyond in the dim oil lamp light.

Sammol was fully dressed, and had his boots on. He pulled on his jacket as he opened the door. "Kiboth is dead," she said.

"And my 'prenticeship is over." She heard the edge of anger in his voice.

"My mother got Kiboth to change his Deed of Intention on his deathbed. *Iceforged* has passed to Thatnog."

"He has disinherited you?" Shock filled Sammol's voice.

"Yes. My mother has arranged a Match for me to Befril Goldbow."

"He is a disgusting old man," Sammol snarled.

"I do not know what to do. And as you are so much better than me at surviving setbacks, I thought..."

As she said those words, she realised what she meant.

Sammol had none of the wealthy privilege of a white-complexioned dwarf like herself. Her cheeks flushed hot with embarrassment, but fortunately he could not see that in the darkness.

He reached to the floor of his room and picked up a pack of his own. Danetha's burden was becoming uncomfortable, and she re-set the pack, easing the straps over her shoulders. "I am leaving too," he said. "And since you seem to have run away, we should go together."

"Where can we go?" she asked.

"Gilvora Blackfinger keeps the Mirek Sailors' Resthouse on the far side of the harbour. She will ask no questions about us, nor permit others to do so. We can stay there for a while until we settle our plans. Let us go."

He heaved his pack over his shoulder, extinguished the oil lamps in the room, and came outside, closing and locking the door behind him. His actions had the air of a plan long-made, and she wondered what had happened to him to cause him to creep from home in the middle of the night. She was so selfish, so wrapped-up in her own story, that she hadn't considered the devastation of her one true friend.

Sammol led her across the garden, making new tracks in the wet grass, scuffing it in circular motions every few steps. Danetha wanted to ask him why, but now was not the time for conversation.

He opened the gate without a creak and ushered her though. They walked in silence along the rough road, Danetha stumbling several times before they reached the fringe of the Froyyim Forest. To her right the lights of Dimiel Harbour burned, and her throat closed up at the sight. She traced the line of berths on the quay. The lamps illuminated the ships at anchor there. There was only one she had eyes for. *Iceforged* was still in port, and the watch set. She could see the dark forms of sailors on his decks. She swallowed hard, forcing down a sob.

The massive loss she had just suffered had not fully hit yet. She was still numb from her mother's news, but she could not afford to wallow in her sadness for long. If she was to stay free she must have a plan.

Sammol led her towards the forest, and she hesitated for a moment. "We will not enter the trees," he said. "There is a path which runs from the forest border to the Resthouse. It is that we must find."

Danetha let him lead the way, and after a few paces he said, "Found it. The path runs direct from here. We must arrive while it is still night."

She did not know why that was so, but chose not to

question him. It was an odd feeling for her privilege to count for nothing, but tonight it did. She would have to get used to her loss of status. It would be her life from now on.

They walked in silence, accompanied only by the sounds of night-calling birds. Once, a white ghostbird swooped down low over them, startling a squeak out of Danetha. But they met no two-legs out here in the black night. They were all safely gone to their beds.

Rest was what Danetha desired most now. She was dragging tired from the exertion of managing the ship and the shocks attendant on her father's death. She had no strength for lengthy explanations to strangers. The walk put her into a trance, the rhythm of placing one foot in front of the other soothing her grieved mind.

Sammol's footsteps halted, and she slowed her pace. "We are nearing the Resthouse," he said. "You must understand that it is a haven for dwarves of dark complexions, and for other species who are often badly treated. Some may be hostile to you because of your father. You must stay hidden in your room until Gilvora decides it is safe for you. Her I would trust with my life."

"I understand," she said. She did not, fully. But she had the first glimmer of how her father's power had protected her. Power she could not rely on now.

They walked on, and in a short while Sammol stopped, then turned right onto a different path. Danetha had no trouble following it in the night-black. It had been worn deep into the surrounding turf and her feet told her where its edges lay. Slowly she followed her friend down the slope until he stopped again.

"We have reached the Resthouse's back gate," he said.

She heard the click of tumblers. The gate had a lock. Sammol eased the tumblers into place and pushed the gate open.

"How did you do that in the dark?" she asked as he ushered her through.

"The keys are cast with runes," he said. "Those who know the old Ogath language would know it."

"I do not know it," she said. "Will I be welcome here?"

Sammol led her forward again. "That we are about to discover," he said.

CHAPTER SIX

Danetha's heart thundered as they traversed the garden paths. There were lamps lit at its margins, showing the way past well-stocked vegetable beds and bird coops. The path led her towards a large terrace paved in rough stone.

Lanterns hung from poles around the terrace's margins, creating a bright pool of light which led towards another gate. At this one, Sammol stopped. "We must wait to be noticed here," he said.

"In the middle of the night? Who will look for us then?" Danetha asked.

"Many of the Resthouse's residents arrive in the dark hours. There are many escaping a bad life."

Danetha had no answer for that. Her father's money had kept her away from such things. The night was cold, and she stamped her feet, trying to get some warmth back into them. How did people live under arches and in alleyways in a winter of the Northern Alliance? That was another thought she had never had before.

The gate swung open and a tall, pale-faced human surveyed them. "Who are you?" he demanded.

"Sammol Blackwind and..."

"And Danetha Windhammer," a female dwarf said

from behind the glowering human. "Let them pass."

The human scowled at Danetha, but stepped aside at the dwarf's command. Danetha swiftly followed Sammol into a well-lit lobby before the human gatekeeper could change his mind and bar her.

"Welcome," the woman said. "I am Gilvora Blackfinger." She was tall for a dwarf, and had skin as black as the night outside. Her hair was streaked with the first grey, and held in many tiny braids by filigree silver beads. This was a dwarf who exuded power.

"Thank you," Danetha said. "I am sorry to drag you from your bed at this late hour."

Gilvora laughed. "Night is the most usual time for my family of fugitives and misfits to arrive. Shut the door, Quashawn," she said to the human. The man did as she bid, and when he turned towards Danetha again his scowl was gone.

"Let me find you rooms," Gilvora said.

"Thank you. We can pay," Danetha replied.

Gilvora reached out a weathered hand and placed it over Danetha's. "Such things are for later. I have heard the news of your father. For now, you will need a soft bed and an absence of company."

Gilvora's kindness brought tears to Danetha's eyes.

"Thank you," she said again. "That would be most welcome."

"Follow me." Gilvora crossed the lobby to a narrow staircase at its end. Danetha climbed the staircase behind her, the effort taking the last of her strength. When Gilvora showed her into a tiny room and bade her sleep, Danetha had just enough energy left to remove her boots and clothes.

She settled into the bed, surprised at how fine the linens were. It was her last thought before oblivion took her.

When she woke, daylight seeped around the drapes which closed off the window. Danetha yawned, and stretched out in the narrow bed. It might be small, but it had proved very comfortable, and she had slept long and well.

She rose and dressed, then made her way out to the landing. Several other doors led off it, no doubt leading to other sleeping rooms. She considered going in search of breakfast, then decided it was wiser to stay hidden in her room and went back inside.

Shortly after, a knock at her door startled her. "Danetha?" a voice said. It was Sammol. She opened the door to see him standing in the hallway with Gilvora behind him.

"Good, you are dressed," Gilvora said. "Bring your things and come up to the attic. Befril Goldbow has organized a search you. It will not be long before he comes here."

"How dare he!" Danetha snarled. "He has no rights to me. I am a free woman."

"And you shall remain so if I can arrange that. You must go up to the attic and hide until Befril has departed. The best way to ensure your safety is to show him that you are not here."

Danetha slid on her jacket, picked up her bulky pack, and followed Gilvora to the narrow flight of steps at the end of the hallway. Their host showed her and Sammol into a large attic room. Light flooded into it through many skylights. The room was set with tables and chairs, and the two tall end walls were fitted with substantial closets.

Gilvora led them to one of the end walls and opened the door of a tall cupboard. It had no shelves inside. She stepped into it and slid her finger along a recess in the back panel. Danetha heard a click. Gilvora pulled the panel forward, revealing a room beyond it. It was furnished with soft chairs, and there was space on the floor to dump their packs. A skylight in the centre of the roof let in bright daylight.

"Hang up your jackets," Gilvora instructed, indicating the

row of solid brass hooks on the far wall. Danetha pulled off her jacket and hung it up.

"Let me show you how the lock works from this side," Gilvora said. "But it would be best if you waited here for me to collect you."

When Danetha was certain she knew how the lock worked Gilvora shut them in. Danetha sank into one of the stuffed chairs, pummelling its seat with her fists until it made a comfortable shape.

"So now we wait," she said.

Gilvora was a friend and ally of Sammol. But would that allyship extend to her in the face of Befril's bluster? Would the dwarf betray her?

CHAPTER SEVEN

Danetha waited in silence for a long time, trying not to make any noise. She was just beginning to think that her imprisonment was a joke by Gilvora when she heard voices beyond the cupboard.

"You said this room was not used regularly. Then why is it set with tables and chairs?" The man's voice was pompous, and Danetha thought his question rude.

"That is really no business of yours," Gilvora said sharply. "But out of courtesy, I will answer. You are a Merchant, Befril, so you have no connection to the ocean." Danetha admired the subtlety of the insult. It was likely the man would not even know he had been insulted. "Where do you think the poor rescued sailors who survive a shipwreck in our fierce winter seas are brought? We Resthouses are the only places with sufficient space for whole crews at such short warning. This is where I house them."

"Humph," he said. "You have an odd collection of residents."

"I consented to allow you to examine my establishment," Gilvora said. "I did not consent to receiving insults from you about my guests. All are equally welcome here, and as you can see now we have examined every room, Danetha

Windhammer is not here."

"Then show me out, woman."

The voices receded, and Sammol turned to Danetha. "Your mother would match you to that monster?" he asked.

"Yes. Which is why I had to leave."

The lock of the false wall clicked, and Gilvora beckoned them out. "The bore has gone," she said. "You are safe now. Stay up here, and I will bring you breakfast."

Gilvora departed, and Danetha paced the attic room, peering out of the skylights. All she could see were squares of dull grey sky. The Northern Alliance autumn was asserting itself today.

Their host returned, leading a human into the room. He had the tanned complexion of the Marisol Isles, and the tray he carried was heavily laden. He put it down on the nearest table, sighing in relief.

Danetha thanked him, and removed the dishes from the tray while Gilvora retrieved plates and cutlery. "Eat," she said. "Fill your bellies."

When Gilvora had gone Danetha investigated the offerings. Eggs, cured meats, grains, and sausages all found their way onto her plate. She had been too exhausted to be hungry last night, and this morning's panic had suppressed her appetite too, but now it had returned in full force.

"I have been so selfish seeing to my own needs that I have not considered why you chose to accompany me here," she said to Sammol between mouthfuls of delicious food. "What are your plans for the future? I will understand if you no longer consider me a good friend after your dismissal by my father."

His gaze caught hers and she began to fidget under the scrutiny of those dark eyes. "Nothing has changed between us, Danetha. You are not your father's actions." He took the last bite of his sausage, and reached for another from the dish. "I was hoping you would come to find me, for I needed to leave my home too. My mother had arranged to Match me to Nordoma Duskbrow."

"Oh," Danetha said. The Duskbrows were a rare thing: a black-complexioned family of Merchants who were as rich as the richest white-complexioned families. How had Rura managed that match? Although, in all fairness, Nordoma could never be described as beautiful.

"Rura wanted the wealth her family would bring." He looked away from her. "My mother is not doing well. Buzum is greedy, and has cut her allowance recently. I will not be

Matched to Nordoma. Nor does she wish to be Matched to me. Nordoma prefers the company of women."

"So we have both left home," Danetha replied. "The question now is how we spend our lives in the future."

CHAPTER EIGHT

Before Danetha had time to consider her future Gilvora reappeared, leading two female dwarves. They both had very pale complexions, and hair the colour of silver.

"These are Thova Whitewind and Menna Icedelver, sailors from Jamica," Gilvora said. "They wish to speak with you."

Danetha hesitated for a moment, wondering if this was some kind of trap set by her mother or Befril, but Sammol said, "Ask them to join us."

The two dwarves took seats at the table. Both moved with the balance and strength of sailors. They were dressed in breeches and tunics which were well-worn, and wore sturdy hide boots.

"Why did you wish this meeting?" Danetha asked.

"Because we wish to ally with you," Thova said.

"If you were thinking to take ship aboard *Iceforged*, you should know that my father has disinherited me." A spike of pain jabbed at Danetha's heart when she spoke those words. Informing a stranger of her loss made it hurt more.

"I am afraid that all of Dimiel already knows that," Menna replied. "Thatnog has wasted no time in strutting around the harbour as *Iceforged's* new captain."

Danetha blinked, willing back the tears. She did not want to hear about her boastful brother.

"We would not take ship with him even if he offered," Thova said. "We were Matched in Elexis, where such unions are legal, but there are many who will not accept us. I fear your brother is one of those. We were hoping that, as you two did not accept the fates your families planned for you, that you would be more accepting of us. We have many years of experience sailing both *Hornsinger* and *Fireflyer*, until their captains changed and discharged us."

Danetha knew those ships, both big square-riggers. If these dwarves had sailed them for some years then they would have the experience she needed. "I have no ship to sail," she said.

Thova leaned forward, her gaze intense. Her eyes were of the palest blue, the colour of a winter morn sky. "We know where you could acquire a ship of your own. A lizardship who is waiting for the right captain."

"Where?" Sammol asked.

"The *Seashimmer* lies hidden in a cave several days' walk from here."

"How do you know that?" Danetha asked. She struggled to keep her voice even. She did not want to betray her interest to these strangers.

"We have climbed into the cave where she is beached," Menna said. She exchanged a look with Thova. "We are well-experienced sailors, but neither of us wishes to take on the challenges of a Captain. We were not born into Trader families. We have neither the connections nor the skills to bargain for good contracts. And there are too many Merchants who are prejudiced against our love for each other."

"We suspect that *Seashimmer* would not accept either of us as Captain," Thova added. "You, however, the lizardship would likely consider suitable."

"Is the ship seaworthy?" Danetha asked.

"We suspect not. She is beached hard onto the rocks in the cave, higher than the highest tide rises. She must have used her magic to carry her there."

"It would explain why she is not visible from the ocean," Sammol replied.

"It would indeed." Thova exchanged a look with Menna, who nodded. "The truth is, we are desperate for new berths. We were hoping you were in the same position and would help."

Danetha leaned back in her seat and tried to think. "To be truthful, I have not considered what my course would be yet.

My father only died last eve."

"We will need crew we can trust," Sammol said. "I know their reputations."

"So are you recommending that I hire them, First Mate?"

His eyes widened at that acknowledgement, then he said, "I am. There may be others in this Resthouse we should consider too."

"That's as may be, but we have no ship yet," she reminded him.

He grinned at her. "There is one for the taking in that cavern. Shall we go and claim the *Seashimmer*?"

As she walked along the path Danetha wondered why she had been mad enough to agree to this journey. It was dusk, and the light was fading fast. Thova led the way forward confidently.

They were traversing the rough path to the north of the fine houses of the Merchants' Quarter. They walked quietly. They did not wish to draw the attention of the wealthy Merchants. Danetha knew from her dealings with them that they were ever fearful of losing the fine treasures they had amassed. That seemed like an impoverished way to live to her, but even so she did not want to fall foul of their hired strongarms.

This night they were bound for Airiel Plankcleaver's boatyard, and that caused Danetha some concern. It was the yard where Kiboth had always taken *Iceforged* when the ship needed repairs. Kiboth had been a good client there. What was the risk of Airiel betraying her to keep Thatnog's custom?

She was too well-known in these parts, and it was a disadvantage now. She was glad they were making for Oslen Headland. There she would not be so well known.

But this night she needed to keep her mind on the path ahead of her. Thova had chosen not to take them along the road which led from Dimiel Harbour to the boatyard. There were too many lanterns lit in the private houses and Bondhouses along that length of road. They would be too easily noticed by the guards which the merchants posted there.

Once they had passed behind the back of the last Bondhouse Thova turned south. "We can join the coast road now," she said. "This section is not well lit."

Danetha felt for the weight of her money purse, tucked away in the inside pocket of her jerkin. Unlit roads were often the haunt of thieves who would not hesitate to cut a throat to acquire an unwary traveller's purse. She hoped no thieves would approach their group of people on this road tonight.

They left the lights of the Bondhouses behind them and Thova turned to her left. "We are on the road now," she said. "There should not be anyone unwise enough to drive a windcar in the darkness, but we should keep our guard up."

Danetha thought that was unlikely, but even so they chose to walk along the left margin of the road, so that they could leap onto the soft verge by its side if necessary.

Her senses were heightened, registering every chirp and chirrup and scrape and noise, alert for anything which would indicate an approaching attack. She wondered where Befril would look for her next. Would he think to look in the places sailors frequented after his failure at the Resthouse?

Rage at his arrogance at deciding to search for her rose again. Anger gave her the strength she needed to stride out along the road. The night air was chill and nipped at her nose, but her other extremities stayed warm. She fell into a trance, keeping a steady pace along the level road.

Ahead of her, the lights of Airiel's boatyard came into view in a dip in the road. The dwarf owned a large sprawl of land rising up from the ocean. Large buildings fronted the waterside, covering dry and wet docks for hauling ships out of the ocean for repair. Airiel's yard was always busy, and sometimes Kiboth had had to wait for several days before her craftspeople had the time to do *Iceforged's* repairs.

They took the dip in the road towards a well-lit gate, which led into the shipyard. Danetha had been there many times with Kiboth, and knew that the building where Airiel kept her records and received clients was immediately opposite the gate. Whether she would be awake at this late hour Danetha doubted. She began to fret about how they would gain access to the boatyard.

Thova walked into the light at the gate, and raised her arm. It took only moments for a huge black-complexioned human to come to meet her.

"Who comes to the shipyard at this late hour?" he roared.

So, we have a showman, Danetha thought. He had clearly been hired for his bulk, as few would choose to engage him in a brawl.

"Thova Whitewind and Menna Icedelver bring Danetha Windhammer and Sammol Blackwind to seek sanctuary."

Danetha saw the man's eyes widen at the mention of her name and braced herself for trouble, but instead he barked "Wait here," and strode off towards the lighted building behind him.

Danetha shifted from foot to foot while she waited for him to return. It took some while, but when he did he unfastened the bolts on the gate and let them into the shipyard. "Airiel's apologies, but she has had an exhausting day and needs to rest," he said. "She gave instructions to settle you for the night."

He took a lantern from a hook by the gate and held it out in front of him, lighting the way along a path to a squat building further up the hill. "You will have to take bunks in our workers' quarters," he said.

Was that a challenge in his voice? If he thought the daughter of a wealthy Trader would be discomforted by sleeping in humble accommodations he was mistaken. "No doubt the space is larger than my tiny bunk on *Iceforged*," she replied. "And it has the advantage of not pitching to and fro while I am trying to sleep." She saw his surprise at her answer, then he nodded.

He led them to a long, low building further up the hill. Danetha knew it was one of the several workers' quarters here. Airiel attracted some of the best shipwrights, and was able to pay them less than the best wages, because she provided them with a home too.

Everywhere shipyards were places of refuge for those who fell through the cracks of the world. They could find a place here if they were willing to work hard. Danetha had never expected to be taking such a refuge herself. How swiftly and completely her world had changed.

The room she was shown to was small and plain, but clean. Sammol was given the room next to hers, and she was reassured by the courtesy of his treatment. The room would be most likely bigger than the tiny store he had occupied on *Iceforged*.

Yet again, she had come to a strange bed exhausted in the middle of the night. It was becoming too familiar. She must find some order and purpose for her life soon.

Danetha woke well past dawn, to the sound of knocking on her door.

"Who is it?" she called.

"Sammol. Airiel invites us to break our fast with her."

Danetha dragged her body out of the bed and dressed. She opened the door of her room. Thova and Menna had gathered there with Sammol. "I needed my rest," she said.

"So did we all," Menna replied. "But if you are like me, your next desire is to fill your belly."

"It is. Perhaps you fine people would show me the way?"

Thova grinned, the first time she had done so. Thova was the serious one. Menna was the jester of the pair. "Follow me," she said, and led the way along the hall.

They entered a large room set with tables and chairs,

several of which were occupied by Airiel's workers. There were both dwarves and humans here, of all different complexions. Airiel had been a trusted confidante for Danetha when she was growing up. Airiel had often found her work to do when her mother had schemed to introduce her to some young dwarf. Because she had spent so much time here she had learned to do the common repair work which sailing ships regularly needed.

The cooks had produced a good spread of solid food and Danetha gratefully filled her stomach. Her mind was working through the things she needed to do today when a burly black-complexioned dwarf sat down beside her.

"So where have you come from, my pretty?" he asked. "Those fine hands are far too delicate for shipwrights' work." He moved his chair closer to her, until his shoulder was touching hers.

Danetha stood up and went to sit at the other end of the table. "Who I am and where I come from are no concerns of yours," she said sharply.

The slob grinned at her. "Fussy, are we? Won't last long in the 'yard then."

"And neither will you." Danetha turned around to see Airiel standing behind the pest. "I took you on against my better judgement. It has proved to be correct. You are dismissed, Thosgram Linesplicer. Collect your things and Danar will escort you out of the 'yard."

Thosgram snarled at Danar, but the huge human dealt easily with the dwarf, insisting he go to his room and collect his things then leave immediately.

"You won't get away with this, bitch," Thosgram snarled at Danetha. "I know who you are. Others will send messagebirds to your home."

"Danar, ensure no messages are sent from my loft," Airiel said.

"Yes, mistress." He hustled Thosgram out of the room.

Now Danetha had another worry. If that malcontent told her mother where she was, Befril might appear and try to claim her.

"You cannot stay here now," Airiel said. "When he is outside the shipyard he will find another loft to send his message. We must plan your onward journey immediately."

CHAPTER NINE

Danetha's mind was awhirl as she followed Airiel across the shipyard and into her workroom. She felt a sense of betrayal at the dwarf's words. Here was someone she had hoped would support her, but now it seemed like that support was being withdrawn.

The shipyard owner closed the door firmly on listening ears as Danetha sat down at her desk. "I understand that Befril thinks he can claim you," she said.

Danetha roused from her angry thoughts. "Does all the land know that?" she snarled.

"Many Traders and Merchants do. Some laugh at your mother, some approve of her efforts to secure the Windhammer fortunes."

"But none think on how I feel about the matter."

Airiel sighed, and now Danetha saw sadness in her eyes. And for the first time she saw the lines of mid age on that pale face. Airiel's black hair had been cropped to her ears, and its strands were streaked with silver. The observation disturbed Danetha. She had known Airiel since she was five years old. She had never noticed the dwarf growing older before.

"I was a fortunate daughter," she said. "My father did

not disinherit me. For if he had I too would have been in your position. I have never wanted any mortal's flesh pressed to mine. I understand your resistance to this match. How can I help you to stay free?"

Danetha's anger fled. She was not being betrayed. "Do you know of the *Seashimmer*?" she asked.

"That old myth? I do my best to disabuse people of the notion that the ship is there."

"But..."

"But of course she is. She does not deserve any of the greedy malcontents who would try to claim her. But you would be a worthy Captain of a lizardship. You should have been the Captain of a lizardship."

Danetha felt tears leap to her eyes, and blinked them away. "Thank you. So you know how to reach her?"

"Thova knows the way. She will guide you true. It is not my place to advise a Captain on her crew, but in my opinion you would do well to take on that pair. They are excellent sailors, and do not deserve the hostility they have encountered to their love."

"I had already decided to offer them berths," Danetha said. "I sense that this 'yard is a haven for people running away from the ugliness of this world."

Airiel leaned back in her seat and smiled, smoothing out

the lines around her mouth. "It is indeed. And if on your voyages later you find some who would benefit from sanctuary here, do not hesitate to send them to me."

"I will definitely remember that," Danetha said. It gave her the glimmer of an idea when *Seashimmer* was sailing of how she could find her purpose and live it. But first she had to find and claim the *Seashimmer*. And if she was successful in that, the ship would need repairs.

Despair took her as she realised the enormity of the challenge she had taken on.

"I am thinking that if the ship has beached herself she may need some hull planks replacing," she said. "But lizardwood... I have no idea where I would find that."

"This knowledge you must to keep to yourselves," Airiel said. "Thova and Menna already know of it, and Sammol will be trustworthy so you may tell him." Danetha was intrigued by Airiel's words and listened with great care to her. "You know of Anbarzil Lake?"

"I do, but I have never visited it."

"Those of us who know of it do not draw attention to it."

"What relevance has that place to the *Seashimmer*?" Danetha asked.

"You will need lizardwood to repair her. Lizardwood

comes from sea serpent cases. You will find them there. On the bottom of that lake bed."

"It has always bothered me that we killed sea serpents for our ships," Danetha said.

"No, it was not like that. Back many years, the ocean was much higher. At one time it reached as far as what is now Anbarzil Lake. The name is from the old Indrajit language, which most have forgotten, and it means lizard lake. It was calm and sheltered, and the sea serpents considered it a good place to lay their eggs when the ocean reached that far. Later, the ocean retreated, leaving the lake landlocked but for the Zabion River, which runs into the ocean right by the *Seashimmer's* cave."

"So if the ship needs repair how would we do that?" Danetha asked.

"First, you will need to find a lizardwood cocoon to lift from the lake bed. They are buried under the mud and stone of ages on the bottom. The serpents buried their eggs in that mud, and the growing youngsters created their cases as they grew. When they were ready to hatch they rocked their cases out of the mud, then split them open with their claws to swim to the surface. Then the lake became poisoned, and each season fewer hatched. None have done so for generations now, and even though the lake is now fresh it is certain that all that remain there are dead."

Airiel sighed. "Such a waste of the creatures of Arvinda." She shook her head. "You know that lizardwood ships have hulls of different colours. You must find a cocoon of the same colour as the *Seashimmer* if you wish to repair her. I do not know why, but repairs made with a different coloured case are never as good."

"Have you seen the *Seashimmer*?" Danetha asked.

"No. She remains just a rumour to me."

"How deep is Anbarzil Lake?"

"It is shallow for most of its space. Only the very centre is deep. A freediver can easily work there, and in Thova and Menna you have two skilled divers. They have made their living diving for shelled fish before. They would be able to find a case for you. Then you would need to float it along the Zabian River, and carry it into the *Seashimmer's* cave."

"That is a mighty task," Danetha said. She began to have doubts about its possibility.

"The cases will float once they are free of the mud. We attach ropes to them to steer them down the river. The difficult part is when the river reaches the sea. Then you will need to bring it ashore."

"This will take much planning," Danetha said. She was

reluctant to move on so early, but she understood why Airiel needed to protect her shipyard. The threat of Danetha's presence here being disclosed to Okrene worried her. Airiel was right. She must move on now.

"I will aid you as I can," Airiel said. "No-one expects sailors to travel inland, therefore I will loan you my largest windcar. If you do not mind being crowded together it will keep you safe."

"Oh," Danetha said. "I have never... sailed a windcar."

"Thova knows how. Sammol too. They will take you down the coast."

Just after noon Danetha climbed into the back of the windcar beside Menna. Thova and Sammol sat in the front. Between them they would steer the vehicle and manage the sail.

They set off along the coast road as the day became gloomy. Danetha had never given any thought before as to why the coast road had two different ribbons. She had always sailed this coast on *Iceforged*. But now she realised that the two corridors were because windcars travelling in different directions needed to be kept separate.

The sail moved differently from those of the ships she was used to, and the windcar was able to sail much closer to the wind than *Iceforged* could ever manage. Their progress along the road was swift. There were a few other vehicles behind them, but traffic on the road on this grey, short autumn day was light. Sammol and Thova changed places regularly, one steering the car, the other hauling in and letting out sail.

As the light faded the road dipped down into the town of Lynwen. Thova brought the car head to wind in a clearing at the side of the road, spilling all speed, and put on the brake. "We must decide where to spend the night," she said. "I know of a Resthouse in this town which will take us and ask no questions. It is owned by my cousins Dovala and Jalgath Softhand. They also chose to love each other and leave home."

"It is who they will speak to which concerns me," Danetha said.

"Many who do not want to be discovered pass through there. Dovala and Jalgath will not betray you."

"Then it would be good to find this place," Sammol said, taking the decision out of Danetha's hands.

Thova set the car in motion again, and a short while later turned it off the coast road and onto a narrower road running inland. The car slacked off speed, and Sammol trimmed sail again.

"That is the Resthouse," Thova said, pointing out the white-painted building a little way ahead of them to their left. As the windcar approached Danetha saw an archway with open gates. The entrance led into a large courtyard. Thova steered the windcar expertly under the arch, and Sammol let the sail go as they entered. The windcar coasted to a stop close to the front door of the Resthouse, and Thova put on the brake.

"I will go and ask if there are rooms for us," she said.

Danetha watched her enter the building, and her misgivings returned. She wondered whether she should adopt a new name in the future. But too many people knew her face for that to work. And why should she hide who she was? She had the right to be who she was. She had done nothing wrong.

Thova returned. "We have rooms," she said. "Fortunately, the Resthouse is quiet now." She turned to Danetha. "I took the liberty of booking a private dining room, so we can stay apart from the other residents. Follow me."

Danetha wondered if the sisters expected her to pay for every room they stayed in on this journey. Her money would soon be exhausted if so. They must have a conversation about it later.

The owners of the Resthouse claimed to be part of a

network providing safe haven for anyone with a need to escape their families. They refused Danetha's money for the rooms.

They provided the weary travellers with a hearty but simple supper, which Danetha much preferred to the over-fussy grand dinners she had been forced to endure when at home. Dovala and Jalgath proved to be good hosts, and Danetha's mind was calmer than it had been for days. At least now she knew they should reach the *Seashimmer* undetected, even if she still had no idea of how they would repair the ship.

As she climbed into her bed she remembered a saying of her father's. "Meet one challenge at a time," he had always told her. It was good advice. She knew what the next steps of her journey were now.

A new feeling stole over her. All her life, others had organised her affairs. If it was not the discipline of *Iceforged's* watches, it was her mother's insistence on her attendance at interminable dinners and balls. She had rarely had much time free to call her own.

But now she had to make her own way across the land, and decide how to win over the *Seashimmer*. It was exhilarating to be free. But it was also terrifying.

CHAPTER TEN

They travelled the coast road from Lynwen to Paria, Nydal to Tamra, and on to Garvan. Each evening they stayed at a Resthouse which was part of the network of safe places Thova had told Danetha about. She wondered how much hostility those two women had faced over the course of their union. That was no more right than the idea of forcing her to Match to Befril.

As they ate dinner in the Resthouse on the evening they reached Per Thova said, "We are approaching the *Seashimmer's* cave. Tomorrow we will reach it."

"I suspected we were nearing the place," Danetha replied. She thought their journey by windcar was much easier than on *Iceforged* at some seasons. The caves, and the submerged rocks outside some of their entrances, could badly disturb the Petros Current and make for very rough sailing.

"The *Seashimmer* lies in the easternmost cave of this coast," Thova said. She paused, then held Danetha's gaze. "I do not know how you will take this suggestion, but I will make it anyway. You will need more than us for crew, and you will need sailors who do not dream of mutiny and deposing their Captain of her ship."

"Go on," Danetha said.

"The Treeshaper shipyard nearby is a place we could acquire both crew and help to repair the *Seashimmer*. The owner Thenna Treeshaper knows of the ship. She has guarded her from the attentions of unworthy Captains." Danetha wondered if the shipyard owner would consider her worthy. "There is also the matter of the windcar. We will need to see that it is returned safely to Airiel. Thenna will arrange that."

Danetha was ashamed to admit that she had given no thought to that matter. When she was at home there had always been someone to take care of any task she wished done. How privileged she had been, and how little she had realised it. But she was no longer in that position.

She considered the suggestion. The more people she told of her plan, the greater the risk that someone would try to frustrate it. But it could also bring shipwrights who would know how to repair the *Seashimmer* far better than she did. And, she admitted to herself, this whole business of finding a suitable case bothered her greatly.

"Father would never use that 'yard," she said. "Even when *Iceforged* clearly needed repairs he would limp up the coast to Airiel."

"Thenna Treeshaper has a midnight complexion," Menna said.

Danetha sensed the challenge in her words. Why had she never questioned her father's decisions on this? Captains had many rituals and superstitions associated with sailing their ships, but when Thenna's name had been mentioned she had seen something else in her father's face. Anger, that was it.

What prompted that reaction? Had Thenna scolded him for his words? Kiboth hated to be humiliated by women. No, it was worse than that. It was time to admit the truth about Kiboth, which she had danced around for years.

"My father was an idiot in such matters," she said. "Once, in a vicious storm, he refused to put in for vital repairs there. Even the figurehead pleaded with him to do so. His twisted beliefs nearly killed us all on that occasion."

"I remember," Sammol said. "It was around the time when I was considering leaving the ship for his harsh treatment of me."

"Then why did you not?" Thova challenged.

"Because Danetha intervened. She faced Kiboth down and told him I was not a slave, that I was an equal member of the ship's crew, and that I must be treated so. And Danetha and I had become best friends by then. There are few who understand and accept those who wish no-one to violate their bodies."

Danetha saw the surprise on Thova's face at his words.

"Did you not know that?" she asked.

"I did not. It... changes matters." All the challenge melted out of the dwarf's demeanour.

"I agree that we should seek help at the Treeshaper 'yard. My hesitation was around wondering who to trust there, as I have never dealt with them," Danetha said.

"Thenna, absolutely," Menna said with strong conviction.

"But there is no point in talking to her unless the *Seashimmer* accepts us," Danetha pointed out. "We must face that test in the morn."

Danetha woke with the dawn, which on this day was bright, and had a light wind. She dressed, and sought out the others in their private dining room. The Resthouse was quiet, and they had not encountered the other residents this morning. Breakfast was swiftly consumed, and soon Danetha's mind was turning to her next task.

They collected their packs, and went on their way again. As Thova steered the windcar along the road towards the headland Danetha's mind flicked to the task of the day. Now she was here, she could finally admit how nervous she was about the idea of meeting the *Seashimmer*.

What if the ship would not accept her? She did not

think she could bear that blow to her heart on top of losing *Iceforged.*

A short way further along the road large buildings stood. Their wide doors made it clear they were for the storage of large objects. "We can park the windcar in a garage here," Thova said. "I know the owner of one of them. We are going fossil-hunting on the shore below on this fine morn."

"Now that is a good idea," Sammol said. "I have found many good creatures here. Some I have polished and sold. This is a good day for finding fossils. Have you ever climbed the zig-zag stair, Danetha?"

"No," she admitted.

"Then you will get the chance this morn."

"And now that is settled let us park the 'car," Thova said.

She steered it into the next building and Sammol released the sail. The car glided to a halt. A human of pale complexion appeared, and began an animated discussion with Menna, punctuated by much laughter.

Danetha got out of the windcar and approached the human. He was twice her height, and solidly-built. He turned as she approached. "Ah, Danetha Windhammer. It is strange to see you on land."

"That is what I have been reduced to since I was disinherited from my ship." Over the last few days her feelings about losing *Iceforged* had switched from shame to anger. She would not hide this injustice from the world.

Shock suffused the human's face. "I did not know of that."

"My Mother has other plans for me."

"The ways of meddling parents are many," he replied, surprising her. "How may I help you?"

"How is the beach this morning?" Thova asked.

"Safe, if you are here for a fossil hunt, I think. Low tide is in half an hour."

"Then we had better go and see what treasures we can acquire," Danetha said.

"Look after the 'car well," Menna said, with a cheeky grin. "It belongs to Airiel."

"I will," he promised.

"I will show you to the stairway," Sammol said.

As Danetha followed Thova to the zig-zag stair she counted herself fortunate that she had met these friends. They knew so much about living on the land which she did not.

When she reached the head of the staircase she looked down, and her breath caught in her throat. The drop to the beach was twice the height of *Iceforged's* mainmast. It was a long way down to the shingle below. But it is also not pitching about in the waves, she told herself. She could do this.

Thova started down first, confidently descending the steps, with Menna a few paces behind. Danetha forced herself to step onto the heavy wooden staircase. If she wished to command these people she could not show weakness now.

Fortunately, the steps had been overlaid with rough metal strips which took away their slipperiness, and she found the footing beneath her boots firm. She set her attention to descending the steps, and made her way down to the beach.

When she reached it Menna and Sammol had faced the cliff and were pointing out strata in its rough surface. "We do not want to spend all day at this pursuit," Danetha said. "We must find the way into the *Seashimmer's* cave soon."

"But we will need to have something to show Daraguk as a reason for spending so much time here," Thova replied.

The remark gave Danetha a window into a world of subterfuge which she had never had to enter before. She hated skulking about.

"There," Sammol said, and uncovered a long, curved stone.

"It is promising," Thova agreed. She took her hammer and tapped the stone expertly along its long side. Danetha exclaimed as it split cleanly into two halves, revealing...

"It is a tiny sea serpent!" she said. The find delighted her.

"You have a good eye, Sammol," Menna said. "I have only found one of those before." Was there a touch of jealousy in her voice?

"Then I will give you the honour of opening this one," Sammol said, and handed her another curved stone.

Menna took it eagerly from him, and tapped the stone just as delicately as Thova had, revealing an even smaller sea serpent curled up in its centre.

"This place is magical," Thova said. She drew out a pack from her jacket pocket and slipped the fossil into it. "We have a short time before the tide is at its lowest. Let us use it searching for fossils."

By the time they called a halt to their fossil hunting they had found one more sea serpent and several other creatures Danetha did not know the nature of. "That is enough," she said. "We must find the *Seashimmer* now. Is there a way into her cave from this beach?"

"There is indeed," Menna replied. "It is one reason why we suggested fossil hunting this morning. It gave us a good reason for being here."

"Thank you," Danetha said, recalling how grumpy she had been at the idea originally. "Show us the way."

Thova took the lead over the shingle. It was loose underfoot, and Danetha's boots sunk into it. Thova led them towards a crack in the cliff, and as Danetha grew close she saw a dark passage leading back from it.

"The way is rough underfoot, and climbs for some while before meeting the passage down from the top of the cliff," Thova said. "There is enough light to see your way by – at least, for the first section."

Danetha reached the crack and looked behind her. There was no other soul on the beach.

"We will not be observed," Thova said. "Follow me, and watch your footing."

She disappeared into the darkness, and Danetha heard her footsteps receding. Anxious not to be left behind, she approached the crack. The passage she stepped into was narrow and made her stoop, and the rock under her boots was uneven. She kept her gaze on her feet as the passage climbed. Thova was right about there being sufficient light. Every few paces a crack in the rock lit the way with a stripe of daylight.

The passage ended in a blank wall, but when Danetha looked to her right she saw a staircase running down. Someone had driven wooden eyes into the wall, and a sturdy braided rope provided a handhold. That was worrying. It suggested that someone used this way regularly. There was little light here, and it faded to black a short way below her.

"There are cut steps in the passage." Thova's voice floated

up to her. "Hold the handrope, and feel for each step with your feet."

That would make slow going, Danetha thought, as she set off downwards.

It took a long time for her to reach the bottom of the staircase.   Long before she reached it she heard the booming of the sea. Her father had told her that caves made the sound of the ocean seem louder. When she was ten years old the booming had frightened her. Today her ears recognized the rhythms of a calm ocean, and it was at a distance. Kiboth had not known why caves made that sound, and all these years later, neither did she.

With each step down the light increased, and now she could see a large flat slab of obsidian at the foot of the staircase. Over it was a jagged arch. Through it she could just see the glimmer of the ocean to her right. To her left...

To her left lay the cave. And in that cave lay her future. Time collapsed, and she was as frightened as that ten year old girl again. How would the lizardship receive her?

CHAPTER ELEVEN

Danetha's heart thumped as she turned her steps towards the cave. It was long and shadowed, and at first she could not see the ship in its depths. Then she made out the shape of the stern, and relief hit her. The *Seashimmer* was here.

"There is a rock shelf to the left of you, which leads all the way around the cave," Thova said.

Danetha sensed something in response to Thova's words, a thickening of the air. It was lizardship magic. "We must go carefully," she said. She raised her voice so that the figurehead could clearly hear her. "Lizardships are masters of the ocean. If *Seashimmer* does not approve of us she could raise the waters to drown us."

Thova looked shocked that she would speak that thought aloud. A saying of Kiboth's came to Danetha. "Better the fear out in the open than freezing up your mind." He told every crew member that they must acknowledge their fears, for denial got people killed.

She was acutely aware of the danger of this situation, and it was making her breathless. She took a step forward, and felt herself pushing through a suffocating haze. It is lizardship magic, she told herself, and most of it is illusion. She took in a deep breath, and the feeling of suffocation eased.

"I am Danetha Windhammer," she said.

She had decided that engaging and challenging the figurehead directly was the way to tackle this task. Even though it frightened her. "I have been disinherited from my rightful Captainship of *Iceforged*, and I am sorely grieved by that. I am hoping that you are ready to sail the oceans again with a new Captain."

At first there was no response to her words, then the cave brightened. She also felt warmer. Now she could see that the ship was a glorious aquamarine colour. Kiboth had told her that ships of that hue were rare. The colour was darkest at the stern and lightened towards the bow. Where it met the figurehead's form the colour became the palest luminous tint. It reminded Danetha of summer light on the Blue Pools of Magnar.

The figurehead turned towards her, in that strange supple way lizardships had of looking right over their shoulders. Light burst from it, becoming so bright that Danetha had to shade her eyes to look at it. The figurehead took the form of a slender maiden, her face long and narrow, neither human nor dwarf. It was more like an elf's features, but did not have the pointed ears of that race. Her complexion was ice-white, as was her hair, which fell in long waves across the back of her gown. A gown which seemed to be made from fish scales.

Lizardship magic made it shimmer silver, blue, and deep purple, the colours rippling across the figurehead's form as she moved. She was both beautiful and frightening. This was a most powerful use of the lizardship's magic.

Iceforged had ceased trying to charm her as she grew to her majority, and Kiboth had always gruffly told the ship to "cease that nonsense". He had never been susceptible to lizardship magic. What did *Seashimmer* wish to achieve by this display? Was Danetha supposed to be frightened by it?

She walked towards the ship, picking her way carefully along the rock shelf. The *Seashimmer's* light gave her the illumination she needed to make her way to the back of cave and face the figurehead.

The ship's eyes were silver, and they watched her approach. Danetha's heart thundered, but she could not falter now. If she wished to be Captain of this magnificent ship then she had to earn the figurehead's respect, and the respect of her watching crew. She kept walking, trying to still the shallow fluttering breaths of her chest. She was well aware of the strength of a figurehead, and of the risk she ran approaching within its striking distance.

"You should know, dwarf, that I killed my last Captain." The figurehead looked down on her with a haughty expression.

"The way I heard it, Narrum Swellbringer foolishly set sail into the teeth of a gale," Danetha replied. Thenna had told her the ship's history, and now she was grateful for that knowledge. "*Iceforged* cautioned us against sailing that day, and Kiboth stayed in port. But then, Kiboth was not as greedy as Narrum."

"Few Captains are as greedy as Narrum." *Seashimmer's* voice was cold and otherworldly. That too did not sound like it belonged to any known species. "I know of Kiboth's reputation. And of yours, Captain's daughter. And I am sorry for your loss."

Danetha's throat closed up. She had not expected that. "Thank you," she managed. "Are you willing to take me as your Captain? These would be my crew. Sammol Blackwind served aboard *Iceforged*. Thova and Menna have much good sailing under their belts."

"And many Captains who will not take them aboard," the ship replied.

Danetha was surprised at how well informed *Seashimmer* was. She knew that lizardships gossiped. It was clear that every passing ship was bringing *Seashimmer* the latest news. That gave her hope. It meant the ship had not withdrawn from the world completely, and so far she could detect none of the ship-madness which had driven *Goldwind* to destroy himself in the Deep Swell.

"That is as wrong as my forced matching to Befril," she said. "If I were Captain I would want to offer berths to others like them."

"Now that is a good purpose, Danetha Windhammer," the figurehead said. Her voice had turned warm, and that haughty face transformed with a most beauteous smile. "It is a purpose I could subscribe to."

Danetha held her breath, waiting for the ship's next words. Would she achieve her goal of becoming Captain of this beautiful ship? Or would *Seashimmer* bring her hopes crashing down around her?

CHAPTER TWELVE

"I accept you as my Captain," *Seashimmer* said.

It took a moment for the words to penetrate Danetha's consciousness. She had succeeded! The lizardship had not driven her away. For the first time since Kiboth's death, Danetha smiled.

She approached the figurehead. Taking a deep breath, she reached up towards it. Without hesitation, *Seashimmer* took her hand. Her grip was not as firm as *Iceforged's*, and her fingers were longer and slender.

"Thank you," Danetha said, and her heart swelled with joy.

It was short-lived. " But I am badly damaged," the lizardship said, "and cannot put out to sea until the damage has been repaired. When I beached myself here I did not intend to sail the seas again. Narrum had poisoned my mind against all two-legs. I was weary of the greed and lack of care I saw all around me, and I did not wish to be part of it any more. But your words have shown me that it need not be so. That there can be reasons other than greed to sail the oceans."

That crystallised Danetha's ideas for her Captainship. She would rescue those threatened with unwanted

Matches and take them to places of safety. She would consider carefully the composition of her crew, admit the dark-complexioned, and those whose love was not accepted elsewhere. Her only test for whether they were suitable would be the depth of their sailing experience. She could not imagine how she would make a living from such decisions, but she was determined to find a way.

"I had feared you would be badly damaged," she said. "I will need to bring shipwrights here to repair your hull. And I know that your hull must be repaired with lizardwood."

"Not only lizardwood, but from a case of the correct colour," *Seashimmer* said. The ship's voice had a peculiar waver as she spoke those words. Did lizardships grieve for the death of their fellows? The thought was uncomfortable.

Now her voice took on a tone of boast. "There are few sea serpents of my colour, and even fewer cases. There is only one source for them, and that is Anbarzil Lake, at the head of the Zabion River."

"I have been told of that place," Danetha said. "I confess that the task of acquiring a case and repairing you concerns me greatly. I do not have the skills for that."

"I would suggest you seek the help of Thenna Treeshaper. She I would trust. As would I trust those she would suggest to help you. She has dissuaded many unsuitable persons from searching for me. But I consider you eminently suitable to be my Captain. It is my good fortune that Kiboth's mind was so twisted."

"Thank you," Danetha said. Tears threatened to flood her eyes. "I will talk with Thenna Treeshaper now." She reached up to the figurehead again. "I will return when I have spoken to her."

The figurehead gave her hand a brief squeeze, then released her. Danetha picked her way across the cave to join her watching friends.

"So you have been accepted as Captain," Sammol said. It was not quite a question.

"I have," Danetha confirmed. "*Seashimmer* has suggested I go and enlist the help of Thenna Treeshaper."

"Then that should be our next task for the day," Thova said. "Let us return to the headland."

They made their way out of the cave to the beach. It was still deserted. The tide was rising, and Sammol led them briskly to the zig-zag stair. The effort of climbing the steep steps soon warmed Danetha's body.

Thova led the way to Daraguk's garage, and they showed off their fossil treasures to him. For the first time Danetha wondered why these tiny sea serpents were found here, and why they weren't in cases. Were they a different species?

Daraguk exclaimed over the smallest one. "I have never seen one so small," he said. "But they fill me with sadness too. These are the generation which did not hatch. They are victims of the Great Poisoning."

Danetha was surprised at his words. "But that took place by Gadiel," she said.

"The Poisoning was from the shiverweed slurry the farmers of that region used a generation ago. Winter storms washed the noxious stuff into the ocean."

"And no doubt the great currents of the world moved it about," Danetha replied. "But surely the serpents would be protected by their cases?"

"No-knows why they were not," he said.

"How awful. I wonder how many other creatures were harmed by the Great Poisoning." That was the history of farmers, and Danetha was a sailor and did not know it well.

"Many creatures were harmed," Daraguk said. "But that was a long time ago and you did not cause it."

"That is true. I am chilled after our fossil hunting. I think it is time to seek somewhere warm," she said to her companions.

"I know just the place," Thova said. "In Oslen is my favourite tea rooms. We should arrive after the business of luncheon, and can look forward to a leisurely afternoon tea."

Daraguk helped Sammol to turn the windcar around and ease it out of the garage. They got into the vehicle, with Thova and Sammol in the front again. Daraguk waved them off, and Thova turned the windcar east, along the coast road to Oslen. The winds had strengthened since they stopped at the garage, and Sammol had to furl some of the sail to prevent their breakneck tumble off the road. They made swift speed along the headland, and Danetha sighed in relief when the road dipped down and the winds slackened off.

"Are we bound for the Treeshaper shipyard?" Thova asked.

"We are indeed," Danetha replied. Meeting *Seashimmer* had brought home to her that she needed expert help to get the ship repaired. And perhaps some of that expert help would in time become crew members when the *Seashimmer* finally set sail.

She missed the close-knit crew of *Iceforged*. She missed Umutt's calm, and his endless store of lore too. He had provided the standard above which she must always rise.

The road took a left turn, and the Treeshaper 'yard spread out before them. It was much larger than Airiel's 'yard. Was that part of Kiboth's objection to coming here? Was he only willing to deal with a woman provided she was not too successful? Did a successful dark-complexioned woman threaten his manhood?

Because she did not subscribe to the world of lust and attraction which seemed to drive most mortals, Danetha often missed undercurrents like that. But she could well imagine Kiboth being threatened by the sight of a black-complexioned woman owning all this land.

They reached the front gates of the 'yard, which were open. Thova steered the car inside and over to a space where several windcars were parked. Some of them had lacquered carriages of the most high shine. Danetha had thought Airiel's vehicle fine enough, but it looked dowdy beside these fine examples.

"We will find Thenna in this first building," Menna said. "We have dealt with her before, and it would be best if we approached her first."

"My father's attitude will not endear her to me," Danetha replied.

"Which is why we will speak to her first," Sammol said. "She knows my family well. The Blackwinds have always used the 'yard for repairs to *Darksilver*."

Danetha wondered if all Thenna's clients were black-complexioned. Was it through such seemingly-simple choices as which 'yard to use that prejudice spread?

She settled down to wait for Sammol to return, which he did swiftly. "Thenna wishes to speak with you," he said.

"Then I must not keep her waiting," Danetha replied, and got out of the windcar. She followed her friend over to the building, and into a large lobby. The panels which clad its walls were finely-inlaid with woods of several shades, and she thought some of them would have come from the Southern Dominion. This was a display of power in another form, in the quieter, more subtle, way of women.

It had its desired effect on her. As she approached Thenna's door she felt as nervous as that ten-year-old child taking her first steps aboard *Iceforged*. What reception would she get within?

CHAPTER THIRTEEN

Thenna Treeshaper was an imposing dwarf. She was not tall, but she stood with a regal bearing. Her complexion was very dark, and her face lined with the experience of middle age. Her hair tumbled down to her shoulders in thick curls. Fine braids on either side of her face were dotted with silver filigree beads. Her broad fingers were bedecked with many rings. This was a dwarf not afraid to flaunt her wealth.

"Welcome, Danetha Windhammer," Thenna said. She held out her hand to shake.

Danetha took it without hesitation, and felt the warm, firm grip of those dark-complexioned fingers. She had known people who refused to shake the hand of a dark-complexioned person. She had never fallen prey to that madness. Her friendship with Sammol had shown her that the colour of a person's skin did not matter.

"I have spoken to *Seashimmer*," Danetha said. "She has accepted me as her Captain."

"That is good news. I have spent the last few years denying any knowledge of her location. I am too busy running a shipyard to go hunting for lost ships." There was mischief in her words, but her gaze was shrewd.

Danetha stilled her fidgeting in the way her mother had

taught her, and saw a flicker of recognition in Thenna's eyes. "I have come to you because the ship needs to be repaired in order to sail again. I reckoned you have the knowledge of where and how to find a suitable case to repair her."

"And why should I aid you, daughter of Kiboth?"

"Because I am not Kiboth," she said. "Because I do not share his stupidities. Because Sammol Blackwind is my best friend, and will be my First Mate on the ship when she sails."

Now she saw surprise in Thenna's eyes, and decided to press her advantage. "Thova and Menna will also be part of my crew, all paid under the usual contracts. It will be my mission to rescue others who wish to avoid the clutches of arranged Matches, or who are being oppressed in other ways. I do not know how I will make my living from that, but it is my purpose."

Thenna smiled, and all tension between them was gone. "That is a grand purpose, Danetha Windhammer, and one I will willingly aid you with. What help do you need from me?"

For the next hour Danetha repeatedly blessed her good fortune in winning Thenna over. The shipyard owner displayed a wealth of knowledge about lizardships. Danetha had never known their history. She had grown up with a talking figurehead, and accepted him without question.

"You will need to acquire a lizardship case from Anbarzil Lake to repair her," Thenna said. "She is a rare aquamarine serpent." So, the ship had not been boasting about that. "You will need to acquire a case of the right colour, and I fear they will be few. Do you freedive?"

"We do," Thova said, and looked at her partner, who nodded. "We are not the best, but we can stay under for some time."

"I have done some freediving," Danetha said. "I have not had much practice though, and cannot go deep."

"I can," Sammol replied.

"You will not need to go deep," Thenna said. "Most of the lake is shallow. But you may need to cover a fair distance before you find the right case. Given your stated purpose, I would like to send a group of my people with you. They may all be open to a berth on the ship later, if you so desire."

Thenna paused. "They are not all dwarves. I have two humans I would like to send with you. Two men who committed the sin of falling in love. They are also black-complexioned."

Danetha did not miss the challenge in Thenna's voice.

"That is not an issue," she said. "They will be welcome. Will we face danger on our journey to the lake?"

"Most likely on the way back. A lizardship case is a valuable prize, and there are some who lie in wait to steal them after the hard work of diving for the case has been done. That is another reason to send humans with you. If you are looking for a full crew, many in this 'yard would be interested."

"I would need to meet them first."

"My suggestion is to take them as your party to Anbarzil Lake. You can decide on that journey if you would work together well. It is rare these days that a new ship requires a whole new crew, and there are many who work here because they do not wish to break the bonds of the alliances they have made. As a crew together, they would take far less time to bond than a crew of scattered individuals."

That was something else Danetha had given no thought to. "I confess I had been taking this quest one step at a time," she said. "For if *Seashimmer* did not accept me, any future plans I had made would be wasted."

"I understand that, but now you must give thought to these things."

"I would require to interview these potential crew

members."

"A very wise move. Shall I arrange that?"

"I would be grateful," Danetha replied.

The next morning Danetha woke before the dawn. She had done all of her interviews yesterday, and her chosen team would leave the 'yard with her as soon as it was light.

She and her companions had slept in the 'yard last night, in comfortable guest quarters. Thenna had provided Danetha with much information for their trip to the lake. Danetha had done little overland travel, and Sammol had proved invaluable in providing information about hazards and things she needed to know.

The journey to the lake would take much longer than she had expected. She had also not expected to be riding a pony there. She had never owned one of those, as she had spent so much time at sea, but she had ridden them on visits to her cousin Osse Earthbond. They were a farming branch of the family, with land near Naja. Osse had taught Danetha how to approach the sturdy ponies they used on the farm, and how to ride one. But it had been some time since Danetha had done so, and she knew the journey to the lake would leave her stiff and sore.

She dressed and made her way over to the dining room

where they had eaten last night. The two humans were already there. Ido Okoro and Mikel Asaju were both very dark and very tall, and had quick gestures and ready smiles. She had taken to them instantly in their interviews last night.

Danetha collected her breakfast – a bowl of hearty porridge with the last of the season's redberries sprinkled on top – and went to sit with them. The rest of her party joined them over the next few minutes, all dressed as she was in sturdy boots and tough trousers and tunics. They were in high spirits as they ate, and their optimism lifted Danetha's mood. She had wakened this morning feeling overwhelmed by the enormity of the quest she had set herself.

The party set out from the 'yard an hour later, into a fine bright morning. Yareli was just rising above the topmost buildings of the shipyard as Thenna's gateman let them out of the gate on the eastern side of the 'yard.

Danetha settled herself more comfortably in the saddle, and stroked her pony's mane as he plodded along. Midnight, he was called, and his coat was as black as his name suggested. Thenna said he had a calm demeanour, and so far she had been proved right.

Ido led the party. Thenna had said he had much experience of leading parties to retrieve cases from the lake. His partner Mikel rode at the rear of the group. Both rode large horses which Danetha vowed never to get close to. They towered over her and terrified her. She confessed to being reassured to have the humans' weight and height to aid her though.

A broad level path ran down from the shipyard's eastern gate towards the river. It ended in a slope which dipped right into the waters. The trail which led to Lake Anbarzil branched off it, running alongside the river to the north. That trail too was broad and flat.

Yareli was low on their right, painting shimmering highlights onto the surface of the river. Danetha had to turn her head away from the brightness. Thenna had said they would have fine weather for the next five days. If she was right, they would hopefully complete this task before the weather broke.

The day became tolerably warm for autumn, and they made steady progress north. This first section of the Zabion River ran through flat, open grassland. As Yareli lowered to their west, Danetha began to worry about sleeping out in the open tonight. They would be such easy targets for robbers.

As the star sank towards the horizon Ido brought their

column to a halt. "Is a small grove a little way ahead. Will provide safety and shelter for us tonight," he said. "Most can sleep inside the trees. We will set watches outside."

Danetha insisted on being included in the watches. She had grown up on *Iceforged* and was well used to them. "I have a suggestion," she said. "As we are all seafaring folk we are all used to four hour watches. Would they not make sense here too?"

"They would indeed," Mikel said. "We will adopt them."

Danetha was assigned to Morning Watch, and slept in the grove until then. The fur wrap she had carried with her kept her surprisingly warm, and she woke with only her nose chilled.

Outside the thicket she could see two fires, one on its northern side and the other on its western side. They burned with a steady flame, and she could see Sammol's form highlighted by the western fire.

She was assigned to relieve him, and inquired whether there had been any trouble. "Not yet," he said, "but Mikel heard footsteps a short while ago."

"That is worrying," she said.

"Mikel said he had been expecting them. It is common

for parties here to be followed. He says we are larger than most, and does not expect trouble."

"That is good," Danetha replied.

Sammol left to snatch a few more hours' sleep, leaving her with her worries of attack.

It did not come on her watch, and at its end the first grey light of pre-dawn was lightening the eastern sky. Danetha confessed to be relieved to see the end of the night. Being on the night watches had never bothered her aboard *Iceforged*, but there her world had been circumscribed by the ship's hull. Few were foolish enough to attack a lizardship in the dark hours.

Few were ever foolish enough to attack a lizardship, but on land things were different. There was no boundary here to keep danger out.

Others were stirring now, and Mikel moved about, banking up the two languid fires, putting a kettle of water to heat on one, and a kettle of porridge over the other. The action reminded Danetha of Garil serving the crew of *Iceforged* the best Ayalin blend after a savage blow.

Grief unexpectedly assailed her, and she stepped back from the fire and moved some paces away for privacy. Sammol joined her there a few moments later, his face anxious. "You look troubled," he said.

"I am sad. This scene reminds me of Garil, and of what I have lost."

"Which is why we are on this quest," he reminded her. "You will make a much greater captain than Kiboth ever was. The world will know of *Seashimmer* and Danetha Windhammer."

"Thank you," she said. His words had penetrated her sadness, and now she could go on.

Mikel pronounced the tea and porridge ready, and Danetha collected her breakfast, perching on a nearby fallen tree limb to eat. The warmth of the food helped to ease the chill in her body, and soon they had eaten, packed up their camp, and were on their way again.

To their west the dense Sannat Forest pressed close to the path, and Danetha got the sense that the humans expected trouble to come from that quarter. It made for a tense ride that day, and the ponies tossed their heads and shook their manes more often.

Towards the end of the day they reached Anbarzil Lake. Yareli had dipped down below the dense canopy of the forest to the west, throwing the lake into shadow. Its waters looked black, and as Danetha grew close Midnight tossed his head, then refused to go on.

Mikel dismounted, and went to soothe his horse. "Our mounts are fractious," he said. "They sense the power which lies beneath the surface of this lake."

Danetha slid off Midnight and went to his head to soothe him. She could sense the power that lay here too. Why had Thenna not mentioned it? She began to doubt the good nature of the shipyard owner again.

Something was calling to her, something from beneath the surface of those still, black waters. And whatever it was, it did not feel friendly.

CHAPTER FOURTEEN

Danetha was relieved to see that there was a substantial bothy a little way back from the lake. She would be able to sleep inside in safety tonight. A solid wooden cabin held bunks, tables and chairs, and a large fireplace. Attached to it was a barn where the horses and ponies could be stabled.

She led Midnight into the barn and relieved him of his saddle. The pony blew out a long breath, which Danetha interpreted as pleasure at being rid of his burden. She stroked his nose, then willingly handed his care over to Ido. She 'd never worked with horses and didn't know what they needed.

When she went into the cabin she saw that Sammol had laid wood in the fireplace and was sparking a flame. The kindling flared and the dead branches he had gathered burst into flame. He arranged more limbs on the pile as the fire took proper hold.

Danetha pulled her sleeping fur onto one the platforms then went to help with the evening meal. Dried hopper meat made a tasty stew, with handfuls of the dried herbs and fruits they had brought with them. As she stirred the pot she thought that there would be little to be foraged from this area. That, more than anything, would keep all but the most dedicated away from the lake.

As they ate their meal Ido told them that sea serpents had died in the lake because of the Great Poisoning. When the seas receded, farmers found the land surrounding the lake and the Zabion River very fertile. They had foolishly added shiverweed slurry to their land, and the noxious brew had leaked into Anbarzil Lake, killing the sea serpents cocooning there.

"We are to dive there tomorrow," Danetha said. "Will that noxious stuff not kill us too?"

"Slurry is long gone," Ido replied. "Will not kill you. What kills unwary divers here is the spirits of the sea serpents. Weak-minded are persuaded by them to breathe under water, and drown. You have all grown up around lizardships. Would expect you to be able to resist their calls."

Danetha could not get his words out of her mind that night, and her rest was troubled. She woke several times, convinced that someone was standing over her. But each time she opened her eyes she saw only the fire, and the silent forms of those on watch.

The morning dawned fine. As soon as Yareli rose high enough to cast its warming rays over the lake the divers prepared for their first venture into it. Danetha retreated to the bothy with Thova and Menna, to pull on their supple skin-suits. Made from oxenhide, the suit would give her body some protection from the cold.

She pulled on her hide boots and cap, then donned her gloves. Fortunately, the diving they must do did not require bare hands. When she emerged from the bothy she saw the crew unpacking posts and ropes.

Mikel turned to the divers and said, "We must ensure that we do not keep searching the same area of the lake. So your first task will be to secure posts from which you can string ropes to divide up the area you will search. Once you have dived a section you will tie a red strip to the rope above it, then move on. This is how we found the wreck of the *Silverwind* off Tirzah."

"I have seen that ship," Danetha replied. In Janmali there was a large building housing the remains of several ancient hulls. Kiboth had insisted on taking her there when she first joined *Iceforged's* crew. He said she must understand why people started using lizardships. It had made sense to her then, but now she wondered if he was trying to justify his control of a lizardship. It was too late to ask him what he felt now.

Mikel handed her three slender sticks, and she made her way over to the lake. There were twelve divers, all dressed in the same tight-fitting hide body suits as herself. Her lacings were a little tight, but they needed to be to overlap the sections and keep the freezing water out.

Sammol led the way into the lake, and she saw him tense up as the water reached his waist. He was standing some distance from the shore, and she realised the lake was shallow for a long way. "It is cold, but not as cold as diving from *Iceforged's* stern on a winter day in Dimiel."

Danetha knew what he spoke of. He had dared her to dive there on midwinter's day several years ago. She had never felt such cold from the ocean, or endured such a huge scolding from her mother afterwards.

She followed the other divers into the lake, and reckoned that Sammol was right. This cold was bearable, but that was not what she feared. She was not hearing any whispers from the serpents, but there was a sense of watchfulness here. The spirits of the sea serpents were aware of them. They were waiting, and watching to see what they did. She had no doubt that they would act eventually.

She waded out a little distance and put her face into the water. The lake was shallow, barely deeper than her shoulders, almost too shallow to swim in. As soon as she put her face beneath the surface she saw the uneven muddy bumps of the lake bottom. Unearthing the cases from beneath that mud would be a tedious endeavour.

She placed her sticks in the mud, then went back for more. In a short time the divers had marked out a sizeable area closest to the bank with a grid of sticks and string.

"Now the hard work begins," Sammol said. He dived down to the first square, using his gloved hand to scrape the mud away from the case buried beneath him, then surfaced swiftly. "White," he said.

Danetha realised they only had to scrape away a small section of mud from each case, sufficient to identify the colour of each one. Would they find an aquamarine case swiftly, or would the task take days? There was no way of knowing.

It was on her third foray of the day that Danetha met the sea serpents' challenge. She was searching a deeper area of the lake bed some paces away from the shore when the voices assailed her.

"Come, join us, dwarf sister," they whispered. There were many voices in her mind, a chorus of male and female speakers, all uttering the words in harmony. The sound was a beautiful, eerie music which drew her in. "Your life of pain and strife can be over in one moment. Let the waters in, and become one with us."

It would be so easy to let go of the pain of her father's betrayal, and the equally painful betrayal of her wishes by Okrene. She could be at peace. She...

CHAPTER FIFTEEN

Hands grasped Danetha's arms and thrust her body up into the air. The light of Yareli shone full into her eyes, making her blink. She coughed and spluttered, forcing the water from her lungs. Her mind cleared as she took in a large gulp of air.

"Go ashore," Sammol told her. "Rest up. We will finish this search."

Danetha hated to be the weak link in the chain, but if she was truthful, she was afraid to venture back into the waters now she had sensed the danger. And the fear in Sammol's voice was clear. Her friend was afraid for her.

She waded out of the shallow water, shivering with more than cold. Fear had seized her body. Ido helped her ashore. "Get to the bothy and dress. Have done enough dives for this day," he said.

Danetha was only too happy to do as he bid. Thova helped her to unlace her sodden costume and Danetha dried her chilled and shivering body and dressed. The fire in the bothy soon started to warm her limbs, but her mind would not as easily lose its chill. She did not want to think of the necessity of returning to those waters and their dangerous siren voices tomorrow. But they would have to do so. Their first day had not yielded a case of the colour they needed.

When the last of the divers came ashore Ido doubled the watch. Danetha asked him why as he tended the fire. "This is the most dangerous time of a case hunt," he said. "The spirits of the serpents know we are here for one of their kind, and they will call to us more strongly now."

That was not reassuring. Danetha soothed her nerves by going to check on their mounts. Ido had set a watch on them too. Danetha could not escape a feeling of imminent attack, and wished they could get this quest completed swiftly.

The ponies and horses were calm, and she took comfort from that. They had already been fed their evening rations, and Midnight came easily to her for a fuss. At least the chill waters of the lake had eased the soreness in her thighs caused by riding him. She returned to the bothy and gratefully accepted the bowl of steaming stew Sammol handed her. The food warmed her nicely before sleep.

Some time in the dark hours she woke to the sound of shouts. Beside her, Sammol roused and reached for his knife. "Stay here," he said, snatched up the weapon, and disappeared into the night.

Now Danetha could hear the clash of blade on blade. She

went to the door to listen. The clashes were coming closer, and she wished she had a weapon. Umutt had taught her in secret how to use a cutlass, in stolen moments when Kiboth and Skylar were resting. Both her father and her mother had refused her requests to be properly trained.

Now, as the sounds of fighting grew even louder, she cursed her parents. She cast her gaze around the bothy, searching for something to use as a weapon. In a dusty corner she found it. Tucked out of sight beneath a bed platform were two metal stanchions. She blessed the travellers who had left them here. She picked one up, getting the heft of it. It was heavy, and needed a two-handed grip, but would serve well to defend the dwarves who were stirring behind her.

She looked away from the embers of the fire, restoring her night sight, and went to the door of the bothy. The fighting sounded fierce. She opened the door to see Sammol being attacked by two dwarves. They were driving him towards the bothy wall, slashing at him with their knives.

They were so intent on him that they did not notice her. She moved in, raised her stanchion, and brought it down as hard as she could on the knife arm of one of Sammol's attackers. The sound of bones cracking was sharp. The dwarf howled, and dropped his knife, cradling his broken arm with his other hand. Danetha darted in and grabbed the knife he had dropped, releasing her stanchion and turning the knife towards Sammol's other attacker.

"Leave us alone!" she roared, her voice more like a man's than a genteel lady's. The attackers snarled, and pressed forward again, but now Danetha was able to aid her friend, and between them they drove the thugs to where Ido and Mikel were engaged in fighting humans. For a time it looked like they might be harmed, but eventually they drove the human attackers back towards the trees. The ruffian dwarves swiftly followed them. Danetha heard several sharp cries, which were swiftly stilled.

"Let us get inside," she said to Sammol. "The night is chill."

"I agree. The night is chill with more than mere darkness now," he replied.

When Danetha woke the next morn she learned what Sammol's words meant. With the coming of dawn she could see that six bodies had been left for dead after the fight. Four were humans, two white-complexioned dwarves. They were all dressed in rough-cured hides and fur jackets. Their bellies had been ripped out, and a trail of blood marked where hungry scavengers had eaten the entrails of the dead before being disturbed.

A shiver ran down her back, and she turned away from the carnage. Her mind shifted to the task of the day. That also filled her with dread.

The day was another tedious one of diving and surfacing, finding nothing but black, red, and white cases. They had uncovered every colour but the aquamarine they required. The *Seashimmer's* comment about being a rare colour was in no way a boast. Now, two days into their quest, it seemed more like a warning.

At least the spirits of the serpents were leaving them alone today. She heard no whispers, and none of the other divers seemed to be afflicted either. It was as if the serpents realised they were intent on retrieving a case, and had ceased their resistance.

The tedious hours of this day brought only disappointment until, on the last dive, Sammol surfaced and raised his arm. "Here!" he shouted. "I have found one. A big one."

Danetha was out of the water and dressed in her land clothes by then, so the task of unearthing the case and bringing it to the shore fell to the other divers with Sammol. She was irritated that neither Ido nor Mikel lent their human strength to the dwarves. Instead, they turned towards the trees and scanned them. Danetha realised they expected another attack.

The divers attached ropes to the case, and half-way through that task Sammol surfaced, holding a struggling dwarf. The man was fighting him, urging Sammol to let him go towards the peace. Danetha shivered. He had been bewitched by the serpents in the way she had yesterday. The slipping away of her will still frightened her, and had made for a fractious night's sleep. A sleep not aided by the attack in the midst of it.

Sammol hauled his struggling burden ashore, and the divers with ropes thankfully surfaced safely. Danetha joined the teams on the ropes, to haul the case ashore. Lizardwood was much denser than the hardest hardwood, but strangely, it floated well too. It was a most desirable combination of characteristics.

Sammol and another black-complexioned dwarf came onto the shore to direct the teams. Danetha wore her hide gloves to protect her palms from the chafing of the roughspun rope. It took a fair time for them to haul the case ashore. When it had been done, everyone was weary and ready for sleep.

Instead, Ido gathered everyone together. "Know you most

desire sleep now," he said. "But this is just the time when raiders are likely to return. Put out the fire in the bothy and haul the case inside it. Set fires outside the bothy and stables. Will set larger watches tonight. From knowledge of past occasions, they may come in the night to steal our prize. Must be ready for them."

Danetha was assigned to Middle Watch. She bundled herself up in her sleeping fur and sank into slumber immediately.

She woke to Sammol shaking her shoulder. "The raiders have returned," he said.

CHAPTER SIXTEEN

Danetha reached down beneath her sleeping platform for her captured knife. She curled her hand around the grip and pulled it out, startling the dwarf next to her.

Sammol stationed himself by the door along with one of the other black-complexioned dwarves. At Sammol's insistence, Danetha took up a shadowy place in the corner, hidden but ready to strike if necessary.

Her emotions were all churned up. She did not want her best friend to be put into danger instead of her, but she also knew his command made sense. He had been in many fights over the years, and had been properly trained to use the cutlass which he carried. She had not.

Yells and shouts came from outside as the raiders encountered the people watching for them. The noise went on for some time before someone opened the door.

Danetha took in a sharp breath as a human's shadowy form filled the doorway. "I am Ido," he said, identifying himself. "Fight is over. Raiders have been left for the carrion."

Danetha shivered at Ido's cold worlds. Had he killed them all? He was well-used to this danger. Is this what it took to keep a lizardship sailing? How much blood was on Kiboth's hands keeping *Iceforged* in good heart?

Why had she never learned of such things? She had never been told how the sea serpents had been turned into lizardships. She resolved that she would have that difficult conversation with the *Seashimmer* when she returned to Oslen.

But that was some time and a long journey down the river away. And at this moment, she needed to return her attention to keeping watch, and hoping that no more raiders came in the night.

Thankfully, no more raiders did come in the dark hours. Danetha was relieved at 4 a.m., when the Morning Watch took her place. She was still weary, and went straight back to her bed.

She woke the next time to the rays of Yareli streaming through the open bothy door. She reached for her knife, but the figure who entered was Mikel. He went around the room, shaking the shoulders of those still sleeping, rousing them for the day. Danetha dragged herself out of her sleeping fur and followed her nose outside to the smell of breakfast cooking over the fire.

Ido handed her a bowl of porridge with black and redfruits scattered through it. Danetha's stomach rumbled as she smelled the hint of sweetness, and she took herself off to a nearby log to eat her breakfast.

As soon as they were fed Mikel called them together. "Now comes the exhausting part of the journey," he said. "We must float the case down the Zabion River, which is running swiftly at this season. We will not be able to stop once we put the case into the water. Our journey here was leisurely; our journey back will be much swifter, and sleepless. We will need to ride through the dark hours to reach the shipyard, and we and our mounts will both be exhausted by then. You will want to stop. You cannot, if you wish to return home safely."

Danetha shivered at that unspoken warning. She had expected the journey back to the shipyard to be easier. Mikel's words warned her that it would not be.

They swiftly packed up their camp and put out the fires. Then Ido and Mikel arranged for the roping of the case. They attached two thick ropes around either end of it, and fastened the other ends of them to their horses' saddles. The operation was done expertly by the two humans, and Danetha helped to hold the bothy door back while their horses dragged the case down to the river.

Mikel reined in his horse as he reached the water. "Once the case is in the river we will have to move swiftly," he said. "We will not be able to wait for you, so mount up now and keep pace with us."

The horses pulled the case over to the river bank, and much pushing and grunting by the team got it into the waters. As Mikel predicted, the current was swift, and the humans had to take off immediately to keep pace with it. Danetha scrambled onto Midnight, and with Sammol beside her urged the pony to join the group of riders trotting down the trail.

The river ran swiftly, and at some times during the morning they had to canter their mounts to keep pace with the river's flow. In the late afternoon it turned a bend and the flow slackened off.

"We have negotiated the strongest currents," Mikel announced.

Danetha was glad when Midnight slowed to a walk. She was stiff and sore from riding him again. For hours they had been travelling with the forest on their right, but now the trees ended and the trail ran across the flat grasslands. Yareli was already lowering towards the west, and they were very prominent on the wide open plains.

Ido sent two of the dwarves with the freshest mounts galloping down the trail to the Treeshaper 'yard, to give advance notice that they were returning with a case. Something about that action bothered Danetha, but it seemed like a sensible thing to do.

She fell into a daze as the day waned. The clear sky turned to crimson and orange fire to their west. As the day faded to the grey of dusk Sammol came up to ride beside her. "Ido says we must be alert for raiders where the trail meets the path to the 'yard," he said. "We will have to haul the case out of the river then. He says that raiders often come in from the headland to cause trouble there." Danetha's heart sank. She had hoped that they would be safe when they neared the shipyard.

Dusk came on, and the case-guides changed again. Danetha and Midnight had taken their turn guiding the case a while back. Whilst the river's headlong rush had passed, it was still an effort to keep the case level and guide it down the twists and turns of the river.

They rounded the last bend. Ido despatched riders to find the place where the path from the shipyard intersected the trail. The riders did not go far before they stopped. The bank was only a few pony-lengths ahead of them. The two humans pulled on the case ropes, hauling the heavy log into the slack water on the western shore of the river.

The last of the daylight faded from the sky as they turned their horses to face the shipyard. The ropes holding the case tightened as they stopped its progress down the river. "Haul!" Mikel ordered, and he and Ido urged their horses on. The animals grunted as they took up the load of the heavy case as it came out of the water.

It took some time for the horses to haul the case up the slope and onto the trail. Then, from over to Danetha's right, a man roared, "Hand over the case! We are armed and will kill you if you do not."

Ido dropped his rope and spurred his horse towards the sound. "Out of the way, scum!" he snarled. A heavy thud announced that the horse had hit a body. A yell of pain told Danetha that Ido had used his cutlass on the raider.

Other voices sounded, yells coming towards them. Midnight pranced and whinnied, and Danetha heard the rustle of clothing close to her. She stabbed out wildly with her knife, and it connected with something soft. A yelp told her she had wounded one of the attackers.

"More trouble!" someone called as the sound of galloping ponies came towards them.

These riders carried flaming torches, and were coming along the path from the shipyard. Danetha took in a breath and held her knife out, although what she thought she could do against this much-increased number of raiders she did not know.

This is not fair, she thought. But Kiboth had always said the universe had no favourites, that it was not fair.

Was this the way she would die? At the hands of some miserable raider in the dead of night?

CHAPTER SEVENTEEN

"Ido? Mikel? We are here to aid you," a voice called out.

Curses broke out among the raiders as the torch-bearing riders bore down on them. Danetha saw a dozen men running away towards the coast. The torchbearers pursued them, and she gasped as she saw the lead rider reach the running men and slash at them with his sword. Howls of pain and the sounds of falling bodies followed.

Ido retrieved his rope and said, "Leave 'em to deal with the scum. Should get this case into the 'yard."

The two humans urged their horses on, and the ropes creaked as they took up the weight of the case again. Danetha was about to dismount and join the others to haul on the ropes behind the horses when a torch-bearing human arrived, leading five more of his kind.

"We have been sent to haul the case," he said. He handed his torch to Sammol and directed his companions to get behind the horses and pull on the ropes.

Sammol moved his pony to the head of the line, and lit the way for the case-haulers. Danetha fretted about that. This task was intended to be secret, and the sudden blaze of light had put paid to that.

She kept her concerns to herself and let Midnight choose his own pace along the path to the shipyard's gate. The ponies knew they were home, and as soon as the gate opened they trotted into the shipyard. Danetha was glad to dismount and let Thenna's people lead her pony away. She hobbled over to stand with Sammol. The case was being hauled into what Sammol assured her was one of the shipyard's safest buildings. As it reached the door Thenna appeared, and followed the team inside.

She reappeared a few minutes later. "So, you were successful. How much raider trouble did you meet?"

"Raiders at the bothy, and raiders just now," Danetha replied.

"That is becoming usual," Thenna said. "The raider problem is getting worse. But for now, the case - and you - are safe. I am thinking you will need to use a guest room for the remainder of this night?"

"Will the raiders try to snatch the case from this 'yard?" Danetha asked.

"Not if they wish to retain their lives. Go and sleep, Danetha Windhammer. You have more than earned your rest this night."

Danetha slept deeply and well, and woke to Sammol

knocking on the door of her room. She dressed quickly and went to see what he wanted.

"Thenna wishes a meeting," he said. "It is nearly noon, and we must decide how to proceed next."

What Danetha most desired now was a hearty breakfast to still her rumbling stomach, but she followed Sammol along the hallway without protest.

Her wish was granted when they turned into a small dining room with Thenna as its only occupant. "I trust you slept well?" the shipyard owner inquired.

"I did, thank you," Danetha replied, and Sammol added his own confirmation.

They were served a hearty breakfast of porridge and scrambled fowl eggs, and Thenna let them eat in peace. When they were done she said, "So now a case has been found you must repair the ship. It will take many bodies to move the case to the cave, raise the hull off the rocks, and fit the new planks."

"Have you seen the *Seashimmer*?" Danetha asked. She had not been clear on that from Thenna's earlier answers.

"I have talked with her several times in recent days, after my foreman discovered her there. She now regrets her decision to beach herself and is ready to sail back into the world."

"So what must we do to make her seaworthy?" Danetha asked.

"This is an unusual suggestion, but I will make it anyway. First, choose whom you wish for your crew from my people. Then we will see how to direct the work."

"If you will release them, Ido and Mikel would be most welcome."

Thenna looked surprised. "I had not expected you to want humans on your crew."

"I am not my father, nor do I have his prejudices. In some respects, he was a very foolish man," Danetha said.

"It is a rare Trader who overcomes family loyalty to criticise the decisions of its members."

"Those decisions would have had me Matched to Befril Goldbow for his wealth."

Thenna's face showed disgust, then concern. "I am glad you have told me that. Befril is nothing if not persistent. We must hide your presence here from his informants. Fortunately, I know who his people are, and none of them are in my 'yard at present. I would suggest that you stay hidden while repairs to the *Seashimmer* are being carried out, coming and going in the dark hours between the 'yard and the cave."

She hesitated, then said, "I will share this secret with you. The most effective repairs to a lizardship need more than a case of the correct colour. The planks may be cut and shaped expertly, and expertly fitted, but it is the mingling of the energy of the ship and its chosen Captain which makes the work so secure. You will need you to join your energy to the *Seashimmer's* for that."

"Oh," Danetha said. Kiboth had never spoken of this.

"Your father did not tell you?"

"No." The knowledge that the secret had been kept from her hurt. Had her father never expected her to inherit *Iceforged*? Was his plan always to pass the Captaincy to Thatnog? The betrayal made her heart hurt again.

Thenna reached out and put her dark hand over Danetha's pale one. "What Kiboth did was wrong. *Iceforged* should have been yours. I will do all I can to see that *Seashimmer* sails with you as her Captain."

CHAPTER EIGHTEEN

Danetha knew she would need a bigger crew than the one she appointed that day, but they would form the backbone of her people. Along with Ido and Mikel, she appointed four dwarves as deckhands, and the elf Cirdan Othamar as her Cargomaster. Thenna vouched for them all as absolutely trustworthy. Danetha decided the choice of the rest of her crew could wait until *Seashimmer* was ready to sail. The risk of loose gossip among those she had already appointed was great enough. She did not wish to lose her repaired ship to new raiders.

As the last of the light faded from the sky Danetha and Sammol followed Ido and Mikel through the shipyard to a small gate in the south-eastern corner of the compound.

The gate had a puzzle lock, but Ido dealt with it easily, and soon they were slipping outside the 'yard and onto a rough track which wound down to the caves. Ido led the way confidently in the dark.

"Way into the cave is here. Watch your footing," he warned.

Danetha felt the ground beneath her feet slope down. She put out her hand to steady herself, and touched rock. She put out her other hand, and felt rock on her other side. As she took more steps the path continued to descend, and the rock on either side of her rose higher.

Ahead of Ido, an eerie green light began to glow, outlining the human's form. He did not reach for his cutlass, and so did not consider the light to be a threat, and walked forward into it. Danetha speeded her steps to catch up with him.

The passage turned a corner, and she stopped and gaped at the sight before her. The walls and ceiling glowed with an eerie green light. "What is this?" she asked

"Some kind of tiny creature. Lives in huge mats on the walls," Ido replied. "Lights up in response to our presence. No-one knows why."

That was helpful, but it caused Danetha to fret about others discovering the way into the *Seashimmer's* cave.

"Careful ahead," Ido warned. "Are steps down into the cave, but they are rough rock. You should enter first, Danetha Windhammer."

He stood back to allow her to lead the party down into the cave. Danetha hesitated. Was this some kind of trap? Or was he afraid of the lizardship which lay beyond this passageway?

She would not find out by standing here. She took a cautious step forward, and found the rope handrail she had used on her previous visit to the cave. A blast of colder air told her where the passage from the beach met the stairway. As she had done before, she shuffled down the steps and entered the cave.

The lizardship roused as she approached, and the figurehead looked down at her. "So, you have returned, Danetha Windhammer. Who are these you bring with you?" The figurehead's silver gaze was focused on the two humans.

"These are Ido and Mikel. They led our party to Anbarzil Lake to acquire a case for you."

The figurehead's demeanour changed, and Danetha sensed something from the ship. Was it excitement? "And did you find a case?" she asked.

"We did. Ido and Mikel helped to fight off the raiders who wished to steal it from us. I wish them to be a part of my crew. But more importantly, they have come to see what damage you have sustained."

"I fear it is more than I planned. It will take a shipwright's skills to repair me."

"Ido and Mikel are shipwrights at Thenna Treeshaper's 'yard," Danetha said. She saw her chance to get the ship to accept her chosen crew now. "They will direct the works to repair your hull."

"You may approach, humans. It is some time since I have

had humans treading my decks," the ship said.

"Thank you," Danetha replied as the two shipwrights moved forward. She stepped back to watch them examine the ship.

"You have three splintered planks, *Seashimmer*," Mikel said eventually. "We will have to raise you from the rock and replace them."

"Can the repairs be done?" Danetha sensed hope in the ship's question.

"We have repaired worse damage. And we have retrieved a case of the right colour."

"You must bring it here intact," the ship insisted.

"It is too heavy," Mikel objected.

The figurehead turned her silver gaze on him, and something in her expression caused him to step back. "It is bad enough that two-legs caused the death of the serpent growing there. The least reparation you can make is to bring the case to me to absorb the serpent's spirit."

Mikel looked horrified. "I did not know that..."

"Two-legs do not wish you to know that they have destroyed our memories."

"Most do not know," Sammol said. "I did not."

Danetha was mightily relieved at her friend's words, and went towards the figurehead. She reached up her hand towards it. "We cannot restore what you have lost," she said. "All we can do is give you a new life sailing the oceans. And perhaps we can become your friends too."

She turned to Ido and Mikel. "Can the case be brought here whole?" she asked.

"Have floated hardwood logs into this cave," Ido said. "Case will be more challenging. Will require a barge and some excellent sailing."

"We would need to do this in the dark hours," Danetha said. "We cannot risk raiders noticing us bringing the case in. That makes the operation more dangerous."

"Indeed it does. And we will need to have people here at all hours of the day once the case has arrived," Mikel replied. "The work of splitting it will take some time, and we must work secretly if we are to hide your presence here, *Seashimmer*."

"That is agreed," the ship said. "I will look forward to sailing the oceans again. Bring the case down soon, two-legs."

CHAPTER NINETEEN

It was nearly dawn by the time the party returned to the shipyard. Thenna intercepted Danetha on the other side of the gate, asking for a meeting with her and Sammol right away. Danetha was tired, and desired nothing but sleep now, but agreed to the shipyard owner's request.

"I shall not keep you long," Thenna said, "but we must talk about how the repairs are to be accomplished."

They went to Thenna's office to decide who would be allocated to which repair team, and how they would be paid. Thenna was willing to keep the teams on as paid employees of the shipyard for a time, a generous offer which surprised Danetha.

"In return I would wish you to acknowledge that my 'yard carried out the ship's repairs," Thenna said. "And if you would recommend my services to other captains you meet, that would be most welcome." She sighed. "The Traders' Guild is keen to keep its members mainly pale-complexioned. Buzil Blackwind is one of the few they have admitted to membership. And because most members are pale-complexioned, they look for repairs among their own kind, and are not aware of our talents."

Danetha was ashamed that she did not know that. But

she had not set foot in the Guildhouse since she was fifteen years old, not since Bugol Underbew had lusted after her. Kiboth had refused to take her there after that incident.

"I would be happy to do so," Danetha replied. "Part of my purpose will be to right such injustices."

The next night, as soon as it was full dark, Ido ordered the teams which would haul the case down to the river to convene in the shipyard. When they had assembled he and Mikel had their horses move the case, but this time they did not ride the animals. Instead they backed their horses down to the water, directing the animals with long reins.

At dusk the teams had taken a barge down to the river on a wheeled sled. The ship was a curious craft with a retractable keel, and one sturdy mast which Danetha knew would carry a fair expanse of sail. She had been asked to Captain the ship, for she knew the currents around the headland well.

She had concerns about that, which she aired with Sammol. "This craft is so different from the bulk of *Iceforged*," she said. "And we will be sailing far closer to the shore than Ice ever would."

"That is true, but you do know the currents there," he replied. "Danetha, you must do this. You will have some of your future crew on board the barge. They will watch what you do."

That raised Danetha's worries even more. If she were to miscalculate... Now she realised the difference between a Captain and their First Mate. As Captain, every decision would ultimately be hers. She would not have her suggestions overruled by Kiboth now. The enormity of that responsibility sent a chill down her spine. Could she do this? Was she good enough to Captain *Seashimmer* across the oceans of Arvinda?

She pushed that concern aside and returned to the current task. It took a long time to haul the case onto the barge, and it was nearly Middle Watch before they were ready to sail.

Danetha had checked the weather constantly until dark, noting the cloud formations and the wind direction. Thenna had spoken to a sailor who had brought a small skiff into the 'yard for repair at sunset. He said the currents around the headland were calm and the wind moderate, blowing in a westerly direction. That put wind and current running together, and would call for some swift sail-handling.

They needed to time their arrival at the cave with the highest of the tide, in order to float the barge inside. Danetha harboured the hope that the lizardship would help with that task by controlling the ocean around them. She wondered how often *Iceforged* had saved the ship from the consequences of bad decisions by moving the oceans about.

"Cast off," she ordered when they were all settled. The dwarves on the bank released the lines which had been keeping the barge still in the river. Instantly it picked up speed.

Sammol and another of her crew, the dwarf Alviss Stormmantle, raised the sail, but kept it half-furled as the barge rode the river currents out to the ocean. Alviss had enthusiastically accepted Danetha's offer of a place on her crew, and she suspected the dwarf had often been overlooked because of her womanhood. She would not make that mistake. Talent came in all colours, shapes, and sizes, and she intended to use the best of it, wherever she found it.

"Nearing the end of the river," Ido warned.

Danetha could feel the change in the current, and in the wind direction. "Unfurl sail," she ordered. She pushed the tiller over until the wind was following the barge from abaft the beam. The ship picked up speed, and she sighted the Nur Light, on the headland just beyond Per.

She set Sammol to counting. She knew from sailing *Iceforged* that a count of thirty from the river mouth would take them close to the cave. But she had never tried to enter it, and had never been this close to the coast in the dark hours.

She steered the barge onwards, alert to every movement of wind and tide until Sammol yelled, "Cave ahead!" Danetha gave the order to reduce sail, and pushed the tiller over. She could already feel the disturbance in the currents caused by the change in the landmass.

The barge turned to starboard, and the current slackened off, then the wind. The sound of water slapping against the rock of the cave came to her from straight ahead. The barge was lifted up, and surged forward. Alviss screamed.

The slap, boom, and roar of the ocean was all around them, and Danetha could not make sense of the sounds. Then Ido held his light up and up she saw that the barge had ridden a high wave well into the cave. But they were by no means close enough to unload the case by *Seashimmer*. An expanse of mud lay between them and the rocks on which the lizardship was beached.

"Hold on, little dwarves," the figurehead said.

Danetha grabbed wildly for the mast as the barge surged forward again. The ship rushed towards the jumbled rocks on the cave floor, and she willed herself not to scream. As if *Seashimmer* had heard her thoughts, the lizardship slacked off the wave. The barge descended carefully onto the rock close to the lizardship and stuck fast, without sustaining the least damage. The wave which had borne them into the cave receded. The next one did not reach any further than the cave entrance.

Danetha's knees were shaking. *Seashimmer* had sent that wave into the cave, and controlled it so carefully that neither they nor the barge suffered any damage as it beached on the rocks. It was a most potent demonstration of a lizardship's power, and it frightened her. She had never seen *Iceforged* do anything like that.

She began to wonder if lizardships hid their powers from their Captains. If so, why had *Seashimmer* chosen to show her this now? Was it because she could not get the case in and her repairs done any other way?

Sammol leapt ashore and secured lines around several heavy rocks while Danetha went to the bow and wondered how the case could be got off the barge.

Ido came to join her, holding his light up and looking down over the bow. "Perfect," he said.

"How will we get the case ashore?" she asked, following him down onto the rock.

"Will slide it on a board."

He went to the far end of the cave and planted his brand in

between the rocks by the wall. The other dwarves came ashore, bearing other torches, which they planted at various places around the cave. When they were all lodged they gave a bright and even light over the end of the cave. Danetha realised they had done this before.

She worried about the lights being seen from passing ships, but Mikel assured her they would not be seen from outside.

As he spoke she saw Ido and another of her crew, the dwarf Uze Bronzehand, work to slide the board into place under the case. Uze's skin was dark brown, but lighter than Sammol's, and her hair was long and braided. She took up one of the ropes attached to the case, and determinedly stepped down to the rock of the cave.

Mikel detailed two teams to haul the weight of the board with the case upon it down the ramp and over the rock to the lizardship. As the case came off the barge the figurehead looked over her shoulder and watched them. "Bring it close to me," she ordered.

Danetha wanted to object to the work involved in hauling the heavy case over the rock, but *Seashimmer's* excitement at seeing it stilled her protest. Mikel and Ido came to the head of the rope teams, and with their help the board was hauled over to the lizardship.

The figurehead reached her hands down towards the case. Danetha sensed power flowing from both the figurehead and the case.

"You must be a part of this, Captain," *Seashimmer* said. "You must understand what you will be Captain of. Take my hand."

Danetha hesitated for a moment, and saw the figurehead's face turn to regard her. Those silver eyes seemed to see right through her soul. She had a feeling she was being measured, tested to see if she was worthy.

She reached up and took *Seashimmer's* hand, then at the figurehead's urging placed her other hand on the case. Sound surrounded her, an eerie whispering that was far away and cold-sounding. It was not words she could recognize. Then the sound became words, but they belonged to a language she had never heard before. They whispered all around her, passing from *Seashimmer* to the case, and back again.

Danetha's alarm rose, and she tried to retrieve her hand from the figurehead's grasp, to step away from... whatever was holding her in thrall.

She could not free herself. The figurehead and the dead sea serpent held her fast between them, and she was entirely at their mercy.

CHAPTER TWENTY

The voices halted, and *Seashimmer* released Danetha's hand. She stumbled, and would have fallen if Sammol had not grasped her arm. She turned to him, and saw him gasp.

"What is the matter?" she asked. Her voice sounded strange, as if it had taken on an otherworldly timbre.

"Your eyes..." his words held fear. "What has she done to you?"

Danetha blinked, and the world slid into focus again. "What of my eyes?" she asked. Her voice was her own now.

Sammol studied her face again, his expression anxious. "For a moment they seemed to have turned silver, but now they are their usual blue."

The figurehead turned and looked down at him. "That is the touch of a lizardship," she said. "All who Captain them are changed."

Sammol's expression said that he did not like the idea.

"You two-legs changed us. Your poisoning of the land prevented us from hatching into the sea serpents we should have become. We were meant to be free creatures, roaming the depths of the oceans, not things trapped in our cases. Not figureheads of ships for two-legs to use.

"As you have changed us, the least service you can give is to help return us to the ocean in this different form. As sea serpents we would have been free creatures, now we are not. But sailing the oceans as a lizardship, we can get some measure of that freedom back."

"I am sorry," Danetha said. "We cannot right this wrong."

"No, you cannot. But it is sufficient that you acknowledge the wrong was done. I can find some peace sailing the oceans. I wish you to help me do that again."

The atmosphere in the cave changed, and the figurehead looked away from them. "I have absorbed my sister's memories. Her case is now nothing but dead wood. You may commence my repairs."

The rest of that night was taken up with people coming and going from the shipyard. They brought with them heavy timbers, to construct the cradle which would raise the lizardship off the rock for repair. All night the dwarves and humans of Danetha's crew hauled timbers and equipment into the cave, their actions directed by the elf Cirdan Othamar. Danetha learned that he had directed many such operations to repair other ships here. He would make a good Cargomaster.

When dawn broke the cradle which would support the *Seashimmer* was half-built, and Danetha got her first glimmer of how long the repairs to the ship would take.

Winter set in, and Danetha's trips to the cave became cold affairs. The cradle was completed, and on one night ropes and blocks were suspended from eyes in the cave roof which Danetha had never noticed before. Over several nervous hours *Seashimmer* was hauled onto the completed cradle.

Danetha spent the whole night in a panic as she watched the shipwrights pull on the ropes, lifting the lizardship off the rocks. The hull creaked alarmingly as the ropes took her up, but the figurehead remained calm. Danetha reckoned that if the ship did not panic about the move then there was no reason for her to do so.

Just after dawn *Seashimmer* was eventually settled securely in the cradle, and Danetha went with Mikel to examine the damage to her hull.

There were three splintered planks, all placed beneath the forward hold. Danetha felt irrationally relieved that the ship had not breached her hull beneath the captain's quarters. The planks around the shattered ones would need re-seating, and the whole area re-caulking. Probably the whole ship would require re-caulking.

She began to worry about how far her saved money

would go. She needed to talk to Thenna about the cost of these repairs soon.

By midwinter day the three broken planks had been replaced with new ones skilfully cut to match from the case they had retrieved. The wood of the case was hard to hew, and to Danetha's surprise the shipwrights worked with bare backs to cut it, even on the coldest nights.

She spent many hours of each night pacing the cave, watching them work. She could not understand how they knew which pieces of the case to cut. They had an uncanny ability to see where the natural shape of the case would provide the curve they needed on the cut plank.

The year turned, and the hull repairs were completed. As Danetha inspected them, she could hardly see the difference between the repaired planks and the original ship. The aquamarine of the case they had recovered perfectly matched *Seashimmer's* original hull.

Now came the tedious job of caulking the hull. Mikel and Ido considered that the whole ship required re-caulking, but *Seashimmer* assured them they would not need to do that. "Caulk the new planks," she said. "That will be sufficient."

Mikel nodded, but Danetha saw unrest in his eyes. "Aye, *Seashimmer*. You know best," he said.

The caulking was carried out, and when it was completed the figurehead summoned Danetha to her. "Now it is time for lizardship magic to ensure my hull is watertight," she said. "Approach me, Captain." Danetha wondered what the lizardship wanted, but walked towards the figurehead as requested. "Take my hand, and place your other hand on my hull."

Danetha did so, and immediately felt a surge of power flow through her body. She cried out in fear, but the figurehead said, "Hold tight! This requires both my power and your energy."

Danetha forced herself to keep her hand on the hull. Her heart hammered so loudly it was a drumbeat in her ears. Her body tingled, every limb energized with a strange power she had never felt before. The world of the cave faded as her awareness was sucked into *Seashimmer's* aura.

CHAPTER TWENTY ONE

Danetha became aware of figures moving around her, sounds being spoken, but they were at a remove. She was in some kind of invisible cage where the world outside could not reach her.

As if something had shattered a pane of glass, the sounds of the world rushed in. The power faded from her body, and her eyes closed.

Voices whispered, but Danetha did not know what they said. She lay in a bed, but could not move her limbs. She tried to open her eyes, but could not. She floated in nowhere for some time, sleeping and waking, hearing disembodied voices, until finally her eyes opened and she could see and hear clearly again.

"Danetha?" Sammol came to her bedside, leaning over her. His face was anxious. "Are you with us?"

She blinked to bring his face into proper focus, and tried her voice. "I think so." Her words sounded normal. "What happened to me?"

"*Seashimmer* overpowered you. I have heard of such things, but thought they were mere legends."

Danetha tried to sit up, and found that strength was

returning to her body. Sammol placed pillows at her back, and she saw that she was in the Captain's cabin.

"You lay in a trance for two days," he told her. "We were afraid for you."

"Two days?" The news shocked her. How could the lizardship have affected her so? What had she taken on by claiming her?

Danetha was soon up and about again, fretting over the lizardship's continuing repairs. Although the repairs to the hull were complete, there was still much work to be done to her. All her sails needed inspection, and some required repair. Some of the lines which held them had to be replaced.

She spent most of her time aboard the ship now. She had moved into the Captain's cabin permanently after her spell in thrall, when Thenna had warned her that Befril's spies were prowling around her 'yard.

Danetha did not desire many things, but she did not plan to live with the drab furnishings depicting old sea battles which *Seashimmer's* previous Captain had installed. Thenna told her they had some value, and arranged to have them removed and sent to Oslen, to be sold at auction there. They fetched a fair price, which Danetha gave to

Thenna as payment for the ship's repairs, thus keeping her saved monies intact.

Several pieces of silver and pewter had adorned the Captain's cabin, and after discreet inquires to ensure they were not stolen, Danetha sold those in the markets too. She had no need of fine silver on board, it only became a target for raiders. A ship which was not stuffed full of treasures was much safer on the high seas.

As the spring equinox approached the ship was ready to sail. Ido had inspected her masts, and found them sound. The vault of the cave was high enough not to have damaged them in the ship's beaching. Danetha realised *Seashimmer* had beached herself very carefully. She had not wanted to destroy her chances of sailing again.

She could not imagine what it would feel like to be a creature trapped and robbed of free will by the actions of others. Many times she had been concerned by the conversations Kiboth had had with *Iceforged*. There had been an undercurrent of tension to them. The figurehead had always agreed to Kiboth's actions, but Danetha had sensed reluctance on several occasions.

She vowed that she would never take her ship anywhere she did not want to go. She would not be a Captain giving orders to her ship. She would treat the *Seashimmer* as an equal partner.

It was the least reparation she could make for her ancestors robbing the serpent of her true life.

The day before the spring equinox they prepared to sail. Danetha had finished appointing her crew, and they were now all on board the ship, although she still had two places unfilled. She had had her last meeting with Thenna that afternoon, and was anxiously checking the wind and tide constantly during the daylight hours.

She had just come on deck at twilight when Mikel shouted a warning and reached for his cutlass. Sammol turned to Danetha and said, "Best get below, Captain. We will handle this."

"I will not leave my crew to face danger alone."

"I know you are not lacking in courage, but what if the visitor is Befril Goldbow? What if he has got wind that you are here?"

Danetha shuddered. That would be a disaster, with a few hours still to go before the high tide which would float *Seashimmer* out of the cave. She could not afford to let him see her here.

With an uneasy mind she gave in to Sammol's urgings and went below. Who was her visitor at this late hour?

Whoever it was, they would see the lizardship. She fervently hoped it was not raiders bent on divesting her of the ship. She could not bear to lose *Seashimmer* now.

CHAPTER TWENTY TWO

"Who are you?" Danetha heard Mikel's roar from inside her cabin.

She could not hear the reply to his challenge, and fretted and paced around her tiny day room until Sammol came to speak to her.

"Good news," he said, "our visitors are two dwarves seeking berths on *Seashimmer*."

"Who are they, and how do they know of the ship? Where have they come from?" She was not willing to trust strangers mysteriously appearing in this cave right at the time the ship was due to depart.

"Thenna sent them to us. She vouches for them, and says they will make excellent deckhands. You should interview them."

"What do Ido and Mikel say?"

"They endorse Thenna's assessment."

"Then I had better see them."

She came up on deck behind Sammol, and clattered down the gangplank onto the rough rock of the cave. The two dwarves were some paces away, animatedly talking to Mikel. He saw her approach, and turned to her. "We have some potential new crew members," he said.

"Who are you?" Danetha asked.

"I am Gilva Berylhood," the pale-complexioned dwarf said.

"And I am Ruriel Darkback," the other replied. She had a complexion as dark as Sammol's. "Thenna told us you were about to sail with *Seashimmer*. She sent us to you. Please, Captain, we would like to take deckhand's places on your crew."

"Where have you come from, and what is your experience?" Danetha was determined to interview the pair, despite them coming recommended.

"We sailed on the *Windmantle* until the death of Danor Fireflow. His sun Forhuki did not... approve of our love for each other."

"That trouble again?" Danetha said. If they were being denied berths for that reason she was already disposed to help them. "Tell me of your experience."

The two women had many years' excellent experience on several square rigged ships. They had been forced to move berths three times due to changes of captain who did not accept their relationship.

"Would recommend you take both of 'em, Captain," Ido said. "Will complete our crew perfectly."

"Are you willing to come aboard now?" Danetha asked.

"We are," Gilva said. She indicated the two bundles on the rock behind her. "These are all the things we have. We will not take up much space."

"Then welcome aboard the *Seashimmer*," Danetha replied. "Sammol will deal with your contracts. We sail on the morning tide."

Danetha slept well, but woke early. The high spring equinox tide was due in mid-morning, and she sent Ido to rouse her crew well before then.

Her cook, Divion Meatfire, was at work in the galley already. Danetha could smell cooking porridge and berries when she walked in. Divion was from Magnar, but he had promised to reduce the spices in the food he cooked. Danetha would hold him to that. She found the dishes of that region of the Southern Dominion too spicy for her taste.

She took the bowl of porridge he offered her, and poured herself a mug of tea. There were three hours before high tide, sufficient to fill her belly with a hearty breakfast. Already she was feeling worried. This was her first day as Captain, and she did not even know if her ship would reach the ocean safely.

She finished her breakfast and went out on deck.

Sammol was already there, with Ido and Mikel, organizing both watches to check and prepare the sails. Danetha felt a strange helplessness she had never had before. Getting out of this cave would be entrusted to the *Seashimmer*, and she admitted to herself that she was afraid of that.

"All crew to their posts," Danetha ordered. Her crew took up their positions by the masts, ready to unfurl sail when they came out of the cave.

She had sent Ido onto the beach at regular intervals since dawn, to check on the wind and the progress of high tide. He had told her the current was running strong, and the wind coming from the east. The combination of wind and current with the extra high tide would require some swift sail handling, and added to her worries.

"Hold on, little dwarves," the figurehead called. "I am sending the wave in to lift us out now."

Danetha gasped as a huge wave rolled and boomed into the cave. It was too high, the ship's masts would shatter on the cave roof...

Thuds, thumps, and clattering came from beneath the hull as the heavy cradle burst apart. Someone yelped as they were carried astern at an alarming rate, the jagged walls of the cave rushing by swiftly on either side of them. Now they were out in the daylight, and riding the crest of a strange wave which bridged the cave to the ocean some lengths away.

The lizardship settled into the ocean, and began to wallow as the wave sank back into the waters it had come from. Ido was already roaring orders, and Danetha's crew shook off their terror and efficiently hauled sail. They leapt to the task with an ease and familiarity which reassured her. They had had no time to learn this ship's quirks before their swift exit into these difficult seas. She was reassured that they would make a top-notch crew.

Ahead of her the Nydal light showed, its white painted octagonal shape distinctive on the headland. Danetha was just beginning to relax when Mikel called, "We are being pursued!" Her heart leapt. This was what she had feared. Her fears deepened with his next words. "The pursuer is *Iceforged*."

"Thatnog does not know I am here," Danetha said.

"Someone may have told him," Sammol replied. "And if you do not cover your head he will soon find out. Let me take the helm while you do that."

Danetha bristled at the idea of her First Mate giving her orders, then told herself not to be stupid. Sammol was right, and if Thatnog got wind of her being on *Seashimmer* he could sell that information to Befril. That could make her life very difficult.

She quickly retrieved her hooded jacket from her quarters, fastening it up and drawing the hood tight around her face. She returned to the helm to see *Iceforged* gaining on them. "The fool has too much sail up for this blow," Mikel growled, appearing at her elbow. "He is endangering his ship."

"Oh no!" Sammol exclaimed. "Befril Goldbow is on board." Danetha turned to see him studying their pursuer, his eyeglass raised.

"They know I am here," Danetha said. "Someone in the 'yard talked."

"I fear you are right," Mikel replied. "Your orders, Captain?"

"Your advice, Sammol," she said. "Were I to turn *Seashimmer* into the deep, would my crew handle that manoeuvre well?"

"I am confident they would. But will *Seashimmer* consent to such a course?"

"I shall go and ask her now," Danetha replied, and handed the wheel over to him.

As she made her way to the bow the figurehead turned towards her. "I am proposing to flee over the deep ocean to the Marisol Isles," she said. "Do you consent to that?"

"It is no more dangerous than risks my previous Captains have taken." The ship did not sound like she approved of those. "*Iceforged* has just spoken to me. Befril Goldbow intends to drag you off my decks and return you to your mother."

"How dare he!" she roared.

"He will not have you, Captain. Tell your crew to hold on well. Thatnog would not dare to send *Iceforged* the way I shall go."

Sheer terror engulfed Danetha as *Seashimmer* bucked and rolled. The ship had predicted that Thatnog would not follow them here. She was right, and *Iceforged* sailed on the northern side of them, now with much reduced sail. Danetha got the sense that Thatnog was waiting for her to make some fatal mistake – or to decide to turn away from her risky course.

She did neither. Her crew manoeuvred the ship expertly through the churning waters. Danetha knew that many Captains were afraid of that passage, preferring to sail the Long Circle along the coast of the Northern Alliance, and risk their ships only on the short passages between that landmass and the Southern Dominion. She was sure that Thatnog would turn out to be one of those captains. He would not dare to follow her course.

She was proved right, and *Iceforged* did not pursue them. But over the next two days as her crew battled the winds and the rough waves Danetha constantly questioned her decision to take this route. It was not rough enough to send most into seasickness, but rough enough that the galley was shut down and they were reduced to cold food.

On the fourth morning Danetha was surprised to see a smudge of land on the horizon ahead of them. The waves had slackened off, and she went to the bow in a calm spell. "That cannot be the Inari Isle so soon," she said to the figurehead.

"It is indeed," *Seashimmer* replied. "As your crew were already discomforted, I saw no reason not to speed us along with a little of my magic."

"Thank you," Danetha said. "Have you any advice on where I should dock here?"

"I would suggest Sang Harbour on Tahar Isle. I spoke with *Iceforged* just before he passed out of range. He reminded you to ask your Aunt Avora who she really is."

"I had forgotten that advice. We shall make for Sang." She sighed. "That will make for some hard deck work."

"It will, but you have chosen an excellent crew, Captain. We will arrive there swiftly."

Seashimmer's words proved true, and three exhausting days later the ship eased into her berth at Sang harbour.

On this journey they had no cargo to unload, and Danetha had not yet decided whether she would present herself at the Mariner's Guild and demand membership. She rather thought that would play straight into Befril's hands. The Merchant engaged several Captains to transport his goods, and no doubt had offered generous rewards for information about her.

She intended to take *Iceforged's* advice, and to ask Aunt Avora who she really was. She hoped the answers she received would help her to work out what to do next.

CHAPTER TWENTY THREE

Danetha sought out her Aunt Avora as soon as the *Seashimmer* was safely berthed at Sang Harbour. She turned heads as she stepped ashore with Sammol, and worried that someone would inform Befril that she was here. But unless Thatnog raised his courage to sail the deep passage it would be some time before *Iceforged* put into port here. She should be long gone before then.

Danetha suspected that *Iceforged* would not help Thatnog with his magic. Sometimes a lizardship might not have a say in who became its Captain, but it could refuse to aid that Captain in many subtle ways.

She and Sammol climbed the hill to Aunt Avora's apartment. It was early morning, but Avora was clearly expecting them. She showed them into her comfortable day room.

"Congratulations on gaining *Seashimmer*," she said. "I had heard rumours of her, but had discounted them."

"She had hidden herself in a cave. She beached herself hard and damaged her hull," Danetha replied. She told her Aunt the tale of seeking for a case at Anbarzil Lake, and the way they had repaired the ship.

"Quite an adventure," Avora said.

"We had another adventure on the way here," Danetha told her. "Befril Goldbow was aboard *Iceforged*. He had persuaded Thatnog to give chase to us."

"A double betrayal," Avora said.

Tears leapt to Danetha's eyes. That was exactly how she felt. "Yes. We threw them off by taking the deep passage. Thatnog would not dare that."

"Good," Avora said. "The thought of Matching you to Befril is obscene. Okrene must be desperate."

"I do not care if she is," Danetha replied. "I have exiled myself from my family. *Iceforged* said I should ask you about your origins."

"He did, did he? My family disinherited me too." Aunt Avora's words contained no anger. "Like you, I have only revulsion for the idea of joining my body to another's. I am the eldest daughter of a distant branch of your family, who use the name Windspear. They are Traders who sail several small ships which transport goods profitably around the Marisol Isles. I should have taken over the family business when my father died, but my mother wished to Match me to a rich Merchant instead."

"Is that to be the fate of all women?" Danetha asked. "I will not accept it. None of us should."

"I did not," Avora said. "I too ran away from home. At

a young age I had made a friend of Mageriol Boneknitter. Since early childhood I had a passion for healing the sick. I begged Mageriol to take me on as apprentice, and he agreed. By the time I came to my Majority I had attained a Healer's licence and could support myself."

"Will you aid me to make a living as a free Captain?" Danetha asked.

"Indeed I will. You should know that there are more free Captains than Guild-bound."

"I did not know that. My passion is to free all women and girls to be who they wish to be. But I do not know how I will make a living from that."

Avora grinned. "Then it is good that you sought me out. I do."

Danetha's head was fit to explode with all the things she had learned since she docked here. She now knew that there were many networks quietly arranging to free women. In the last three days Avora had introduced her to many people, and helped her to negotiate paid contracts for the carriage of goods. She had met seamstresses and herbalists, and women Merchants dealing in all sorts of goods which women desired. Most of them were members of the Ladies' Guild, which championed women's interests.

Avora's contacts told Danetha that news of her refusal of Befril had passed all around Northern Alliance society, no doubt spread by Okrene. Unfortunately for her mother, the news of Danetha's disappearance did not have the effect she desired. Instead of making Danetha an object of scandal, the news served as example for other daughters to follow.

Avora told her that many women who had already been trapped into Matches wished to control their fertility. Danetha's cargos would contain many plant preparations which the herbalists had created to prevent conception. She learned that the Mariner's Guild had forbidden its members to carry such 'unnatural' cargo. She was tired of men controlling women's lives, and undertook to be a regular supplier of contraceptive preparations.

She would remain a free Captain, and carry such goods as she saw fit, and ensure the freedom of other women.

Two weeks after Danetha sailed into Sang harbour *Seashimmer* was ready to depart. She was bound for the major ports of the Southern Dominion.

The news that Danetha now Captained the lizardship had caused quite a stir in the Southern Dominion. She had received several bird messages begging her to bring the very cargoes which she had loaded. She felt a rare contentment as she strode down the quay towards *Seashimmer's* gangplank with Sammol at her side.

It did not last long. Before she could reach the gangplank a familiar form bustled towards her. Befril had found her.

"There you are! What do you mean by running away from your betrothed?" He turned to the two armed dwarves behind him. "Seize her."

Danetha's rage kindled. "How dare you!" she roared. Every head on the quay turned to watch their interaction. "I have never been betrothed to you, despite what my mother may have said. I refuse you. Get out of my way. My ship is ready to sail."

"Your ship? A woman cannot Captain a lizardship. You must give up this folly and be Matched."

Danetha found she did not fear this pompous fool now. His portly form was clad in a brilliant green tunic fabulously decorated with goldwork. He was ridiculously overdressed on this working quay.

"*Seashimmer* has accepted me as her Captain. She is a replacement for the ship which I was wrongly disinherited from." Her words were cold and measured. She raised her head, and saw *Iceforged* docked two berths down. The figurehead raised a hand and waved to her.

That action enraged Befril. "I will not be cheated of my bride!" he roared.

Danetha retreated as the two armed dwarves came towards her. She backed into the bulk of Ido. "We handle this, Captain," he said.

Mikel joined him, and they stepped in front of Danetha. The two humans held drawn cutlasses, and looked ready to use them. "We will not allow you to threaten our Captain, scruffy little dwarf," Mikel snarled. "Go back to the hovel you came from, and never trouble us again."

Danetha was surprised by his words, and by the effect they had on Befril. He shrank back from them, more from the effect of Mikel's words than the humans' size. "We know where you came from, you pompous little Merchant. Your money will not buy you the body of our Captain."

"Money should not buy any person's body," Danetha replied.

Befril spat on the quay. "Consorting with humans! That is the lowest of the low."

Ido was incensed by the slur. He surged forward and pointed his knife at Befril's chest. "Your mind is a cesspit. Fine clothes do not disguise that. Get!"

"Hear this," Danetha said, stepping forward again. She raised her head and her voice, so that all on the dock could hear her. "I was never betrothed to you, Befril Goldbow. My meddling mother may wish it was so, to prop up the Windhammer fortunes, but it is not. will never be Matched to you, or any other. I am a free Captain. Go back to the Northern Alliance. I never wish to see your face again."

"Ungrateful wretch!" he snarled.

Danetha tensed, expecting his thugs to make another attempt to snatch her, but instead he curtly ordered them back to *Iceforged*, leaving Thatnog exposed on the dock behind him.

Danetha stalked towards her brother. "I hope you are pleased with your stolen command," she snarled. "If accepting the money of worms like Befril Goldbow is the way you intend to Trade, then you have sunk to the lowest level."

She turned her back on him before he could think of a reply, lifted her head, and walked slowly and deliberately to *Seashimmer's* gangplank.

Something had changed on this dock this morning. She had changed. She no longer feared people like Befril, who hid their weak wills behind wealth and hirelings. She would stand tall and defy such bullies wherever she went.

She turned to the two humans and said, "Sheath those cutlasses. We have better things to do than fight. Let us board *Seashimmer*. We have important cargo to deliver."

SEASHIMMER'S QUEST

After Danetha's refusal to be Matched, she takes *Seashimmer* to sail the ports of the Southern Dominion, in a bid to escape her mother's meddling.

There she agrees to transport contraceptive preparations for the Ladies' Guild, a cargo which the male-dominated Mariner's Guild has refused to carry. At several ports she endures the protests of the Original Seafarers against her "evil cargo". Danetha refuses to let them sway her from her mission to transport the cargoes women need for their freedom.

But as protests from the Original Mariners grow stronger, Danetha must summon up all her courage to defy those hateful men.

SEASHIMMER'S CHALLENGE

After a confrontation with her brother Thatnog, Danetha knows it is time to go home to the Northern Dominion and deal with her meddling mother.

Before she can depart on that journey a man approaches her, asking her to transport slaves. She vehemently refuses. But that evil trade has been increasing in recent months, and Danetha fears that her brother Thatnog may be tempted by the wealth transporting slaves offers.

Danetha knows that a confrontation with her mother is long overdue. She must return to Dimiel to deal with Okrene. And to discover whether Thatnog has turned to evil.

www.ingramcontent.com/pod-product-compliance
Lightning Source LLC
Chambersburg PA
CBHW031305120726
47906CB00003B/901